HEADLAND   COPY £

F   Blake, Jennifer,
BLA   1942-

             Bride of a stranger

$17.95

Discard

	DATE	
	X	

9/09

Once during the night she had been awakened by a scream. She had sat up, her heart beating fast, uncertain if the sound had been real or a lingering remnant of a dream. At the rustle of her bedclothes Justin awoke.

"What is it?" he asked, his voice vibrant with a quiet strength in the dark.

"I-I thought I heard someone cry out," she explained, beginning to feel foolish.

They listened together, then just as she opened her mouth to apologize for waking him for nothing the keening scream came again. . . .

Also by Jennifer Blake

DARK MASQUERADE
NIGHT OF THE CANDLES

BRIDE
OF A
STRANGER

JENNIFER
BLAKE

SEVERN
SH
HOUSE

This first hardcover edition published in Great Britain 1990 by
SEVERN HOUSE PUBLISHERS LTD of
35 Manor Road, Wallington, Surrey SM6 0BW.
First published in hardcover format in the U.S.A. 1990 by
SEVERN HOUSE PUBLISHERS INC, New York,
by arrangement with Ballantine Books,
a division of Random House, Inc

British Library Cataloguing in Publication Data
Blake, Jennifer, *1942–*
    Bride of stranger.
    I. Title
    823'.914

    ISBN 0–7278–4052–5

Distributed in the U.S.A. by
Mercedes Distribution Center, Inc
62 Imlay Street, Brooklyn, New York 11231

Printed and bound in Great Britain by
Bookcraft (Bath) Ltd

Chapter One

THE GALLOPING MUSIC of the *contredanse* swung to a halt, and Claire de Hauterive, breathless and flushed from exertion and the heat of the room, sank gratefully onto a satin-covered settee. Her partner seated himself beside her and, unfurling the tiny fan that hung on a ribbon from her wrist, began to fan her vigorously.

"Idiot," she said amiably, laughing at her cousin as she rescued the fragile ivory sticks threaded with pink ribbon.

"You must be overheated," Jean-Claude protested, "I am going up in flames. If you won't use it, then fan me!"

His face was red, his collar points, which had begun the evening in crisp white splendor reaching nearly to his eyes, were sadly wilted, and he did look unbearably hot in his black evening coat with its black satin collar. She took pity on him.

"Not so hard! You will undo all my valet's ef-

1

forts," he said, touching his heavy, intricately arranged cravat. "How do you like this hair style? It is called *le cavalier*."

"That is exactly what it looks like—as though you have been out horseback riding bareheaded. I don't think anything I could do would harm it."

"Claire!"

He relaxed, a grin slowing curving his mouth. "Wait until we are married. Then I will teach you to show a proper respect."

Claire gave him a warm smile before she turned away, her dark gold hair catching the gleam of two hundred candles. The prospect of marriage to Jean-Claude held no alarm for her. She had known for years that they were expected to wed. She was an orphan, the ward of her uncle, Jean-Claude's father, and completely dependent upon him. She and Jean-Claude were of the same age. What could be more natural than that they should marry and live in a portion of the house on Royal Street? Among the Creoles of New Orleans, cousins often married. It would be an undemanding life. Jean-Claude's mother would not allow her to worry herself about the running of the house. She and Jean-Claude liked each other, and if it was now only a brother and sister sort of affection, well, marriage would change that. After the second or third child Jean-Claude would, no doubt, install a quadroon mistress for himself, as most men did, and she would not object too strenuously because it would mean that she would not be as likely to have to bear a child every year. It was all very practical and convenient. The wonder was that they were not married already. Eighteen was very nearly an old maid for a girl, nearly time to throw her corset on top of the armoire, as the saying went. But Jean-Claude's mother felt that eighteen was too young for a man to be tied down. She wanted him to make a grand tour first, but the war in Europe had, so far, made it impossible. Napoleon had been mewed up on St. Helena for several months, but Jean-Claude's mother, remembering the little Corsican's escape from Elba, refused to allow her son to set sail for France until she was sure that the English had him fast. Napoleon, she knew, was Jean-Claude's hero of the moment, and she had a lively fear that if hostilities broke out again her son might feel compelled to join in the fray.

If the prospect of marriage and her life afterward seemed flat and unexciting to Claire, she did not think of complaining. Too many of her friends had been affianced to strange men who carried them off to their homes far from New Orleans into the unknown and dangerous reaches of the bayou country, to plantations surrounded by primeval swamps, and virgin forests. Some had married widowers with several children whom they were expected to mother, or older or unattractive men whose only recommendation was the money that lined their pockets. Jean-Claude was at least familiar, young, and handsome in a boyish manner, with his chestnut curls, long-lashed brown eyes, and olive complexion.

"Look!" Jean-Claude, leaning close, suddenly hissed in her ear.

Following the direction of his slight nod, she swung her gaze toward the door.

A man stood in the doorway, just relinquishing

his hat and cane to the Negro butler behind him. He was tall and dark, and his tailor had not needed to resort to padding to achieve the superb fit of his evening coat across his shoulders. His white shirt and cravat were severely plain, in contrast to the dress of the other men in the room, many of whom wore rows of ruching on their shirt fronts while a few still clung to lace-edged sleeves and cravats.

"Who is he?" she whispered.

"You mean you don't recognize—no, no, of course you don't," Jean-Claude answered himself. "Justin Leroux hasn't made his bow in polite society in ten years at the least. He is the best swordsman and the worst rake in New Orleans. I daresay you have heard of him, at any rate? Saints! Our hostess will be on her head. What a thing to have happen to her carefully arranged *soirée*!"

Claire cast her cousin a questioning glance, searching her mind for some memory of the man, but nothing came.

Near her there came a whisper in the sudden hush that had fallen over the company.

"As handsome as the Angel of Darkness—"

It was a woman's voice, and though it was not an expression Claire would have thought to use, the words found an echo in her mind as she stared at the averted face of the newcomer. His features seen in profile were perfectly formed; a strong chin, classically straight nose, deep-set eyes, and a broad forehead. But dissipation marked his face and his mouth was set in severe lines, almost like those of endured pain. It was difficult to say how old he was, but he must have been more than thirty if what Jean-Claude had said was true.

As if the intensity of her gaze had drawn his attention, Justin Leroux looked directly at Claire as he turned. Staring into his hooded black eyes, whose thick lashes hid his thoughts like a veil, Claire did not at first see the other side of his face.

A murmur ran around the room. Their hostess signaled frantically, and immediately the five musicians seated on a dais in one corner of the room struck up a quadrille.

Claire felt the color draining from her face, but she could not force herself to look away, though she was aware of the furtive movement as an old lady—one of the chaperons seated on a chair near her—made the sign of the cross. It was as if she were under some form of compulsion, her body would not obey her will. Slowly a feeling of cold despair crept over her, and the mantle of an old guilt settled over her shoulders. Compassion held her in its grip. Though she had been enjoying them a moment before, the loud music and the people moving into their positions to dance now rasped at her nerves. Half of her mind recognized this feeling of pity, recognized the empathy that caused it, while the other half rejected it with a kind of horror. Then, slowly, the horror faded and she was left with desolation in her heart.

"Claire—" The touch of Jean-Claude's hand on her arm released her. She shuddered on a long breath and dropped her eyes. There was a tightness in her throat and the pressure of unshed tears against the back of her eyes.

"The mark of Cain," she murmured, without realizing she was speaking aloud.

"For God's sake, Claire. Keep quiet. Two men

have died, another been crippled for life, and a half-dozen more bloodied for saying less than that. But I thought you must have heard of Justin. Few can forget a man who killed his own uncle in a duel, and a mighty smoky meeting at that."

"He can hardly issue a challenge to me," Claire said, trying valiantly for a return of their light banter.

"No," Jean-Claude agreed in a troubled voice. "But Justin has always had the temper of the devil, and little respect for women. Also it must have been some time since he has associated with a *jeune fille*."

"Really, Jean-Claude! But is it true? Is that really a mark of Cain?" She spoke softly, for her cousin's ear alone. And she could not keep her gaze from returning to the scar carved into the right side of Justin Leroux's face. It began high on his cheek bone and curved down the lean side of his cheek to his chin, a white crescent very like the letter *C*.

"Of course not. He has had the scar since he was a child, that is one thing everyone is agreed on. I don't know him that well—above my touch, I'm afraid. I don't fly with that group; haven't the feathers, not to mention the years. Anyway, maman would fall into strong hysterics if she heard I was even seen with his set, much less—"

"What is going to happen now?" Claire interrupted him abruptly. She had noticed several women turning their backs on the man in the doorway, their chins high with indignation.

"Nothing will happen. Didn't I tell you Justin is the best swordsman in the city? Not a man in this room would dare to give him the cut direct, including me! If our host is wise—yes, you see? He goes toward him. Good manners will do the rest, I think."

"Yes," Claire said, slowly letting out the breath she was holding. What had she been afraid of? She was not sure, and yet there was something about the man that told her instinctively that the social barriers that insured good behavior held little meaning for him.

"What troubles me," Jean-Claude mused, "is why Justin is here. He has avoided all social contact for so long, one can only suppose him to be turning over a new leaf—or hanging out for a wife."

"A wife?"

Her cousin shrugged. "Well, consider. Why else would he make the effort? What is there here in this gathering that can not be had in much more comfort and with more gaiety at the quadroon balls on St. Ann Street. The answer? A respectable young lady, a suitable *parti*, for marriage. But enough. Would you like to dance again. This one is slower, a *courante*."

"No, I think not, *mon cher*. Ask someone else, if you like."

"I wasn't anxious to take the floor," he replied, inserting a finger into his cravat and tugging to loosen it. "Are you sure you feel well? Dancing is usually your greatest pleasure. And you had the oddest expression on your face just now, when Justin walked in."

She colored a little, but did not attempt to deny it. "I—I can't explain it to you," she said, her brown eyes thoughtful. "But as I looked at Justin Leroux,

I felt this terrible pity rise up inside me. It was frightening."

Jean-Claude stared at her and she returned his look. She knew she sounded distraught, and yet she had only spoken the truth. It was too much to expect her level-headed cousin to understand.

"Hrumph!"

The sound, so close, startled both of them. They looked up to see their host standing before them, with Justin Leroux at his side.

"A thousand pardons Mademoiselle de Hauterive," he said, coughing apologetically, "but Monsieur Leroux desires to be presented to you and to your cousin. I beg leave to present to you Monsieur Justin Leroux of Sans Songe plantation and the city. Monsieur Leroux, I have the great honor of making you known to Mademoiselle Claire de Hauterive and Monsieur Jean-Claude de Hauterive." Having completed the formal introductions, he bowed and, muttering something about his wife, departed with suspicious alacrity.

There was a small silence. Justin Leroux studied Claire, a measuring look in his black eyes. Claire could feel a flush rising on her face, and she sensed the interest directed at them from all sides. Then he smiled, a chill movement of the lips that was without humor, and for the first time Claire saw the anger that flickered beneath the surface of his calm expression.

Had he heard what she and Jean-Claude were saying? It did not seem possible above the noise of the crowd and the music, but she had no idea how long he had been standing there.

"I believe it is now proper for me to request the

privilege of this dance," Justin said, then turned to the man beside her. "—that is, if you have no objections," he added, one brow arched in mocking inquiry.

"I had only just refused my cousin," Claire said quickly, before Jean-Claude could speak, knowing that he could not deny the courteously phrased request without risking a disturbance.

"Oh," Justin asked smoothly, "what has that to do with my invitation?"

"You—you must see that it would not do for me to accept an invitation to dance with one gentleman in the face of another whom I had refused?"

"I am certain your cousin would understand."

"I believe not, m'sieur. You see, he is also my fiancé." She smiled as she spoke, certain that she had made him an unanswerable excuse.

There was a flicker of appreciation in his eyes, then he turned to Jean-Claude. "This is so?"

She was aware of her cousin's speculative glance at her before he made Justin a half bow from where he stood. "Yes, m'sieur," he agreed.

"She wears no betrothal ring."

"No, it has not been formally announced."

"Then the wedding is not imminent?"

Once again, Jean-Claude was forced to concede this was so.

"You will not mind, I know, if your bride-to-be dances with me. It is such a small thing."

There was an undercurrent in his voice that even Claire could not miss. She saw the corners of her cousin's mouth tighten. She knew that in spite of what he had said, in spite of his respect for the other man's reputation as a swordsman and his prowess on the dueling field, that he would defy Justin Leroux for her sake if he thought she really did not wish to stand up with him on the dance floor.

Jean-Claude spoke. "It is possibly a small thing to you Monsieur Leroux, but it is what *ma cousine* wishes that is important."

"Well spoken," Justin said, outwardly affable but with a trace of steel in his tone. "Then I take it I have your permission if I can but obtain the lady's?"

"Oh, very well!" Claire exclaimed, as she saw her cousin's face grow grim. Rising, she placed her hand on Justin's arm and allowed him to lead her out onto the floor.

The *courante* was a graceful dance much like the stately minuet that had fallen from favor, though without the excess formality of the latter. It was possible to speak to one's partner as one went down the room. However, having gained his object, Justin did not seem inclined to talk. They turned at the end of the room, and Claire, now on his left arm, slanted a glance at the side of his face. Seen at close range, the scar was not as startling as she had first thought. The sun-bronzed skin around it was smooth, the thin line of the scar itself was white and only faintly puckered just beneath his eye where the wound must have gone deeper. No, it was the contrast between that injured cheek and the perfection of the rest of his face that had caused that feeling of outrage and sadness, as though she had witnessed the results of wanton destruction.

The couple ahead of them looked back over their shoulders. The man nodded at Justin, but the woman sent Claire a look of such displeasure that she was reminded once again of his position, or lack of it, in their social circle. It was a reminder also of her fear, fear that had given him the ascendancy over her will.

"I believe it was mentioned that you have a plantation. Is it far from New Orleans?" she asked in a brittle voice, determined to behave in the correct manner.

"I expect you would think so," he answered, gravely following her lead. "Sans Songe is nearly a day's ride from the city."

"Sans Songe; without illusions, a strange name."

"It was called Fleur de la Pois, originally, which means the pick of the lot—the best. My father changed the name several years after his marriage."

She flashed a look at him, caught by some unidentifiable emotion in his voice, then looked away again.

"Is it a large place?" It followed that it must be if it enabled him to keep a residence in the city also.

"Fairly. It takes a good bit of acreage to grow sugar cane. It is good land, bottom land, near the bayou La Beau."

Claire shivered a little. Bayou country. Deep, dark forest, snakes, alligators, prowling animals, far from civilization. "You—you like it there, at Sans Songe?"

"Yes, of course, and so would you, once you knew it."

"I very much doubt it," she said fervently.

The music was slowing to an end, Claire noticed with relief. She swept her partner a deep curtsy, holding it as the last strains died, then started to turn away.

"Wait," he commanded, touching her arm with the tips of his fingers. She raised her eyes to his, startled by his peremptory tone. He indicated one of the french windows that stood open to the cool night air. "Let us walk out onto the gallery for a few minutes."

"I—I couldn't."

"I fail to see why. I am not, after all, such a dangerous character, despite what you have been told. And I would like to further our acquaintance."

"I meant I couldn't without my aunt's permission. It isn't done."

He frowned with impatience, then swung around to stare at the line of dowagers sitting on the chaperon's chairs against the wall on one side of the room.

"Your aunt is—"

"The lady in puce satin," she replied, pointing out her aunt who was staring at them, a scowl on her plump features.

"She looks a veritable dragon," he observed. "I don't believe we will require her permission."

"But I can't—" Claire began, but did not finish, for Justin grasped her wrist and swung her deftly out through the door. Short of causing an undignified scuffle or screaming for rescue, there was little she could do.

Retaining his grip on her wrist he walked along the gallery, or veranda, away from the open floor-to-ceiling windows, toward the end where only a dim light penetrated the darkness.

"You see? You did not need permission."

"But she will be very angry."

He snapped his fingers, shrugging slightly.

"That is all very well for you. You will not have to listen while she berates you with your lack of appreciation for her kindness, or be read a lecture on correct behavior," she told him through compressed lips.

"Come, Claire, don't be waspish," was his only comment.

"I don't believe I gave you the freedom of my name," she informed him.

"No, I took it," he said without concern.

"You—" She could not think of a word that adequately described him.

"Yes?" he asked politely.

"You—you are a barbarian!" she managed finally.

"Am I?"

"You forced me to dance with you—yes, you know you did! You dragged me out here under the very eyes of my chaperon. Why? Why me?"

"Because," he answered, slowly moving closer and taking her forearms in a firm clasp. "Because you felt—how did you put it? 'A terrible pity.' Pity!"

For some reason the anger that she could feel rising in him by the tightening grasp on her arms calmed her own rage.

"Is that so bad? That I pitied you?"

"Pity is the last thing a man wants from a beautiful woman, the very last!"

"I—I'm sorry," she said, her voice a thread of sound.

His fingers dug into her arms so savagely that she gasped and winced. He would not let her go, and she could feel his gaze burning on her lips, could sense some fierce conflict within him.

Suddenly behind them there were footsteps on the gallery floor.

"Claire! What are you doing out here without my consent? It is disgraceful, I am shocked at you. And you, sir? What have you to say?"

Justin dropped his hands to his sides and sketched a creditable bow. "Madame de Hauterive, I believe," he said. "My pleasure. The circumstances are—unusual, and therefore you will perhaps allow me to introduce myself. Justin Leroux, at your service. As to what I was doing, why, Madame, I was persuading your niece to listen to a proposal of marriage."

Jean-Claude's mother made a strangled sound in her throat. She opened her mouth and then shut it. Watching her aunt, Claire did not immediately perceive Justin's words.

"Proposal!" Madame de Hauterive cried.

"What?" Claire asked stupidly.

"Exactly," Justin said, satisfaction in his voice.

"But—but you cannot do such a thing. You must not even think of it. Claire is betrothed to my own son. And in any case," she went on, catching her breath, "it is not done in this manner. You should apply first to my husband, her guardian, through an intermediary. Not that my husband would dream of allowing your suit!"

"Would he not? I wonder why?" Justin said softly.

"Because of what I have just said. Claire is already betrothed, and because—because—" the older woman spluttered to a halt, not quite daring to bring out the reasons that burned on the tip of her tongue.

"I don't believe I find that a satisfactory reason," he insisted with dangerous quietness.

Claire's aunt drew herself up, "I do not have to explain myself to you."

"Come, Claire. You will return with me to the ballroom where you belong."

It was odd, the reluctance that seized her as her aunt beckoned imperiously, staring down her broad nose.

"It is just as well," Justin said, and Claire saw him nod, an abrupt movement in the dim light. "But you may tell your husband that I will wait upon him at eleven of the clock tomorrow morning."

"You may be sure I will tell him, but I am not at all certain he will receive you."

"It would be most unwise of him to refuse me."

Madame de Hauterive stared at him, but she did not comment. "Well, Claire," she said in a hard tone as she turned and marched away without a backward glance.

Catching up her skirts, Claire hurried after her aunt. At the french window she paused to look back at the man standing with his hands clenched at his sides. He gave her a slight bow that made a mockery of the polite gesture.

"Your servant—Claire."

The words whispered across the space between them filled with a meaning she could not comprehend, and yet they touched a chord of response that made her afraid. Turning abruptly, she followed her aunt's wide back.

Justin Leroux did not reenter the house, though Claire kept watch, surreptitiously, on the entrance from the gallery. It was possible that he had returned by a different way and wandered into the cardrooms, but when he did not appear for supper at midnight, she had to suppose that he had gone.

Though Jean-Claude wanted to stay on until the company broke up, it was a relief to Claire when her aunt decided to depart soon after supper.

Claire did not sleep well. She woke several times during the night, caught up in strange nightmares that she could not remember, but even as they receded she was left with a strange inclination to weep. Toward dawn she fell into a heavy sleep. The morning was far advanced when her maid woke her with the cheerful morning call of *"A la café!"* and the rattling of the rings that held the mosquito *baire*, or netting, around the bed as she pushed it aside.

"Drink up your coffee, mam'zelle," Zaza told her as she handed her the cup and placed an extra pillow at her back. "There is a man with your aunt in the salon. She asks that you dress quickly and come to her there."

"A man?" she asked the quick-moving little maid.

"Yes, mam'zelle. A Monsieur Leroux. Do you know him?"

A tremor of unease ran over her. She had not expected Justin to carry out his preposterous threat. This morning the scene on the gallery seemed to lack reality.

"He—is he alone?"

"Yes, mam'zelle."

"And with my aunt, not my uncle?"

"Yes, mam'zelle. Your uncle and Monsieur Jean-Claude went to the market this morning to purchase a brace of snipe for dinner. You know how particular Monsieur de Hauterive is about his game courses."

Claire nodded, uncertain whether that was good or bad. But it was obvious that her aunt had not told her uncle to expect Justin to call, as he had warned her to do. Her uncle must, then, still be ignorant of what had taken place the night before. Contrary to Claire's expectations, her aunt had not poured the tale into her husband's ears on the way home. She had fallen into a thoughtful silence. She had not cared, Claire thought, for the rumors she had heard over the years about Justin Leroux, nor had she liked Claire's explanation of how she had come to be dancing with such an unprincipled rake, especially as it had involved her son. Her aunt had waited until they were alone in Claire's room before beginning the stricture on her conduct that had embroiled Jean-Claude in the contretemps.

Swallowing her coffee, Claire swung her feet out of bed with sudden resolution. "Lay out my blue muslin," she instructed, glancing down at the bruises from Justin Leroux's hands that stained her forearms, "the one with the long, straight sleeves. And hurry."

She tapped on the door of the salon and, bidden to enter, stepped into the room.

Justin Leroux stood beside the cold fireplace, one booted foot resting on the brass fender that sat upon the hearth, and his arm along the mantle. As she entered, he looked up and straightened, staring at her across the room with a look of triumph in his black eyes.

Her aunt, seated on a velvet-covered settee before him with her hands clasped in her lap, rose to her feet and came toward her. She held out one plump beringed hand to Claire, her face gray and suddenly old under its dusting of rice powder.

When Claire placed her fingers in the older woman's hand, her aunt led her forward, and with a ceremonious gesture, gave her hand into Justin's keeping. His fingers closed, warm and firm around hers, tightening as she instinctively tried to withdraw from that intimate contact.

"Claire," her aunt said in a voice that held a faint quaver, "this is your future husband."

Chapter Two

CLAIRE STOOD PERFECTLY still. She looked from Justin to her aunt.

"Well, girl. You needn't stare so," the other woman said looking away, deliberately turning her irritation on Claire to banish her own feeling of guilt.

"I—but I never expected—"

"Nor did I, but M'sieur Leroux has given me an ultimatum."

"I don't understand."

"It is simple. You may have heard the rumors of the affairs of the *maître d'armes*, the so excellent swordsmen who make their living teaching the young men of means to defend their honor with the rapier? They have superior skill with a blade, much superior to the average man. Because of this any woman they choose, even those of high birth, can be theirs if they are ruthless enough. They have only to threaten to call out the lady's husband, or her father, or some other male relative for whom she cares. Most are very discreet. To have such things widely known would be bad for the *maître d'armes'* livelihood. He need not fear his victims. No woman would speak of such an experience, and no man would admit to being afraid to meet the *maître d'armes* on the field of honor. Neat, you will agree."

"Yes, but—" Claire tried to object, bewilderment in her voice.

"This man," she waved toward Justin, speaking of him as if he were not there, "has taken a leaf from their book. He knows that he cannot approach your uncle in the usual way. His past deeds, the lack of esteem in which he is held, his manner of living, and his too obvious contempt for society would make it impossible for my husband to consider his suit if he should press it according to custom. But he is aware that few men in New Orleans can hope to defeat him in a duel, indeed few of the *maître d'armes* would care to cross swords with him. And so he threatens to force a meeting upon Jean-Claude, unless you are given to him."

Jean-Claude. Young, even-tempered, with little interest in sword play beyond what was considered fashionable and necessary for a young man among the *beau monde*. He would not have a chance.

Claire felt a chill move over her body. Even her fingers, still in Justin's clutch, grew cold. Slowly but firmly she withdrew them.

"He is clever, your future husband. He realized that if he approached Jean-Claude, my son would surely accept his challenge. And he suspected, quite rightly, that my husband, if applied to, might feel that it was a point of honor not to give in to his blackmail. But I, Jean-Claude's mother—" She stopped, unable to continue for the rage and chagrin that choked her. It was obvious from the look of hate that she sent Justin that it was difficult for her to behave civilly toward him, despite her fear for her son.

"I—I can't do it," Claire said.

"Can't? Of course you can!" her aunt exclaimed. "Would you rather Jean-Claude died at this man's hands? He will kill him, Claire. He will kill my son!"

"But what of Jean-Claude and me? We are betrothed."

"It is not yet official. There will be talk, yes, but it is unavoidable in any case with such an alliance." The older woman gripped her hands together and began pacing back and forth in her agitation.

"But what could I say to him, and to my uncle? How could it be explained?" Claire recognized the desperation in her own voice and tried to control it. Her fingernails were cutting into the palms of her hands and slowly she forced herself to relax.

"We—we must say that it is a *grande passion*. You would be desolate if you were not allowed to marry your Justin. You must make it convincing. I am certain M'sieur Leroux will play his part." Her aunt flung him a sarcastic glance. "As for your uncle, I will manage him. He always had a tender place in his heart for your dead father, his brother, and for you. He will wish you to be—happy."

"Please," Claire said, looking only at her aunt. "Surely there is some other way?"

"Would you rather see Jean-Claude spitted on this man's sword like a capon? That is the only other alternative! Oh, no, my girl. You will stop this quibbling at once. You should be glad that it is marriage this man has proposed, for regardless of your maidenly shrinking you will do as he requests. You will be wed in the cathedral as soon as it may be arranged, before Lent, as M'sieur Leroux desires. And don't give yourself any 'die away' airs in my presence. You are not the first girl to be married to a man who is personally distasteful to her, nor will you be the last."

She shot a vicious look at the man beside Claire. Justin's face was a mask of controlled rage, and the scar on his cheek stood out like a red brand.

"I think that will do," he said, staring at her aunt through slitted eyes. "I wish to speak to Claire alone now, if you please." He held up a hand as her aunt began to object. "I realize, though you might not believe it, that it is not done, but I find I am tiring of hearing of what is allowed and what is not. Surely the conventions no longer matter?"

"Apparently not!" the older woman answered. She looked at Claire for a long moment. Then her face hardened and she left the room, closing the door with a snap behind her.

"You should be glad it is marriage this man has proposed—"

The words lingered in Claire's head. They, more than anything else her aunt had said, proved to her how hopeless it was to try to escape the trap that had been set for her. But they did not give her confidence for this moment. Staring down at her hands, examining her cuticles without seeing them, fretting the edge of her sleeve where it covered her wrist, she thought of the night before. She remembered her first sight of Justin across the shining floor of the ballroom, of their dance and their stiff conversation, both on the dance floor and on the gallery. What had there been in that brief meeting to warrant this elaborate scheme? Was it, as Jean-Claude had suggested, that Justin wanted a wife, one of respectable birth? Perhaps having found someone he considered suitable he did not intend to waste time on a long courtship, or trying to convince her guardian of his worthiness?

"Well, Claire?" Justin interrupted her thoughts. "I rather thought you would appreciate this opportunity to relieve your temper."

"Why?" she asked, turning to him abruptly.

"Because I was certain you would be in a towering rage. You told me last evening that I was a barbarian. I suspected you were longing to assure me that I had lived up to the name. Aren't you?"

"No—yes—I mean, what I intended to say was, why did you do it?" she explained, ignoring his comment. "And why did you ever mention marriage so suddenly last evening? Was it so important to pay me out for pitying you?"

He smiled, a brief quirk of the corner of his mouth. "My reason is much simpler than that. I wanted you—" he said, and watched the color that surged to her hairline before he added, "as my wife."

"But to threaten murder," she exclaimed in confusion.

"You seem to forget that my opponent would have a fair chance of killing me."

"An equal chance?"

He did not answer for a moment, then he said, "We need not consider that, I think, since your aunt will see to it that Jean-Claude never comes to the point."

"I can't believe you would actually meet my cousin if I refused you."

"You think not?" He stared at her, a frown drawing his brows together. Then the frown disappeared, his eyes grew cold and his face seemed to harden. "It scarcely matters what you believe. It is what Madame de Hauterive believes that is important. And she obviously is determined that I shall not be allowed to touch so much as a curl on her precious son's head, no matter what it costs you."

"Don't. Please," she whispered, pain at the truth in his words knifing through her.

"Claire—" he said quickly, then he caught her elbow and pulled her toward him without gentleness.

"It does no good to mope and repine," he went on with a harsh note in his voice as he gave her a little shake. "Be angry. It is the best protection from the pain of what must be faced. Don't let anyone beat you down—or make you cry."

She wondered fleetingly how he had known she was so close to tears. She stared up at him, but though she blinked hard she could not keep them from filling her eyes and spilling over to tremble on her lashes.

"Perhaps this will rouse you to wrath," he said, and drew her into his arms. His lips came down upon hers with a burning pressure, branding her with his seal of possession.

For one stunned moment she was still, then she pushed against his chest with her hands that were trapped against her. He stepped back a pace, but did not let her go. Critically he surveyed the indignation that glittered behind the tears in her eyes, and caused her breath to move quickly in and out between her parted lips.

"Much better," he observed. "I have no liking for weeping willows."

"Do you not?" she said tightly as she twisted her shoulders from his unresisting fingers. "Your likes and dislikes must, of course, be an object with me?"

"I believe it is usual when two people are to be wed."

"Very true, if there is some degree of—of tenderness, or respect, between them. I do not foresee that there will ever be anything between us but resentment and—and hate."

"What? No pity?" His voice mocked her attempt at reason.

She turned away abruptly, her face cold with dislike. She moved to the door and pulled it open, then with her hand on the knob, swung around.

"No," she said in a hard voice. "No pity."

She closed the door quietly behind her.

The wedding arrangements went forward with what seemed to Claire an indecent haste. In less than a week the engagement breakfast—the *dejeuner de fiançailles*—was held, and under the somewhat skeptical eyes of her aunt's relatives and the friends of the family, the traditional betrothal ring of a ruby in a flat yellow gold setting surrounded by diamonds was placed upon her finger.

Following that happy event, Justin went into the country to his plantation to inform his family of his approaching marriage. His absence relieved Claire of the necessity of entertaining him of an evening and removed the possibility of the many parties that would have been given to celebrate their coming nuptials. He returned when two weeks had elapsed, and the morning after his return the *corbeille de noce*, a basket of gifts from the groom arrived. It contained a handkerchief edged in lace as fine as cobwebs, a fine hat veil of lace to screen her complexion from the sun and a fan of white silk edged in lace and marabou tufts and with sticks inlaid with mother-of-pearl. There was a cashmere shawl in a delicate shade of blossom pink, so fine it could be pulled through a ring, two pairs of kid gloves with meticulously set-in fingers, a comb for her hair with gold and mother-of-pearl inlay, a cameo of Louis XVII, and a pair of earrings, pearls shaped like teardrops.

Madame de Hauterive helped Claire unpack the basket, exclaiming as each treasure was lifted from the tissue paper. And before she took the basket away to the salon to be placed on display she sent Claire a thoughtful look, her eyebrows raised. "He doesn't appear to be a clench-fist," she said.

Claire was forced to agree, but she had no enthusiasm for the gifts. The arrival of the *corbeille de noce* was a signal. Three days more to the wedding. Three days during which time she was not allowed to leave the confines of the house.

"Claire, wait!"

She turned back at the foot of the stairs to let

Jean-Claude, leaving the salon behind her, catch up with her.

"I haven't been able to talk to you," he complained, "since this whole thing came up. You are always surrounded by women, seamstresses, milliners, mantua makers, and maids rushing around with armloads of trousseau linens. And if it's not that, it's my mother guarding you, or at least it seems so. I'm forever being told to take myself off."

"Poor Jean-Claude. I suppose we have rather pushed you around from here to there," she said with a quick, nervous smile.

"It isn't that—"

"You aren't feeling—hurt, are you?" She covered his hand where it rested on the newel post, a coaxing smile in her eyes.

"Perhaps a little," he agreed with a wry grin. "You are a beautiful girl. I had grown used to thinking of you as mine, and was quite looking forward to being your husband—in a few years' time."

"I rather thought France and the tour mattered more. I am sorry I won't be here to wish you bon voyage."

"Yes, so am I, and I'm glad I am to go abroad at last, but that isn't—"

"Are you put out then at being jilted? Have your friends been saying things you don't like?"

"I've had a few nudges and the odd look or two, but nothing to signify, not if you are happy. But that's just it, Claire. Are you happy? You seem pale and thinner, not at all the blooming bride-to-be. Is—anything wrong? I mean—I know I am putting this clumsily, but I am concerned for you. I have this feeling there is something you are not telling."

"Don't be absurd," she said, smiling into his brown eyes, touching with the tip of one finger the earnest frown between his thick brows. "It is just that everything must be done at once, before Lent. I am a little tired, and I suppose all brides are a bit on edge. It seems so strange, to be leaving all of you and going away to live with people I have never met. But I expect I will soon become used to it— with J-Justin's help." How hard it was to say his name so casually while the very thought of what lay before her filled her nights with distress.

"You are sure? Mother assures me it is a love-match, but I thought you quite disliked the man on sight."

"Did you not know that love often begins that way?" she said, forcing a light laugh.

"Fickle, that's what you are." His face relaxed. "A cruel jade, leading men on. I should count myself lucky to have escaped from your toils."

"Indeed you should. I would have led you a merry dance, always reminding you that we are of an age and interfering in your affairs. But, of course, if you prefer to arrive in Paris posing as a young man with a broken heart to make yourself interesting, I have no objection to being the villainess in the piece!"

He grinned. "A tongue like an adder! You will be lucky if Justin doesn't break your neck for you if you give him any of your fine *parole*."

"Yes—" she answered, but the smile curving her lips did not reach her eyes.

Her wedding day dawned with thunder. It was so dark in the room that Zaza, her maid, had to light the night candle standing on the commode table before she brought the coffee tray to her bedside. Half-way through her breakfast it began to rain, a slashing downpour that rattled on the roof and beat against the great leaves of the banana tree in the courtyard outside her bedroom window. It was still raining, though at a more gentle tempo, in the afternoon, when the hairdresser was shown into her room.

The woman, Madame Elspeth, was a mulatto of middle age, with dark piercing eyes, and with her hair decently covered by a madras *tignon*. She carried the tools of her trade about with her in the pockets of a voluminous overall apron, and at once commandeered the dressing table and began to lay her tongs, pomade, heating frame, pins, and pot of lacquer out upon it. The heating frame was unfolded and set up over a candle, then the tongs were placed upon it. Claire was urged forward to the chair before the mirror with profuse compliments on the beauty of her abundant, freshly washed hair, a linen towel was placed over her shoulders, and the ordeal began.

First her hair was parted in the center and then drawn back to the crown of her head. Small curls were snipped short at the temples and cheeks and deftly curled with the tongs, then touched with just a suspicion of lacquer. The extra length of her hair was formed into a chignon at the crown, with the free ends being formed with the tongs into masses of shining ringlets that fell down the back of her head. A crown of orange blossoms was then carefully placed on the coiffure with a few of the curls gently teased forward to curl artlessly around it.

"C'est magnifique!" the hairdresser exclaimed, stepping back and clasping her hands in ecstasy.

"Most becoming," her aunt said grudgingly, a little frown touching her forehead as she surveyed the hectic flush that glowed on Claire's cheeks. "Take care that you do nothing to disturb it. Madame Elspeth must come to me now, and it still lacks an hour or more before time to begin dressing. You might occupy yourself in the meantime with overseeing the packing of your bandboxes. They have been left to last. Monsieur Leroux has requested that they be placed with your trunk on the traveling coach as soon as it arrives."

"Yes, of course," Claire answered, slipping the towel from about her neck and rising to her feet. Her hats and veils were all that was left in the great armoire that took up one wall of her room, except for her wedding gown. She moved to open the great doors of the armoire and lift the hats down while the hairdresser gathered up her tools and her aunt waited impatiently with her hand on the door knob.

"Ah," the hairdresser said as the door swung open, "the wedding ensemble. May I not see?" She glided forward to stand beside Claire.

The gown was of white silk muslin with small puff sleeves and a low scooped décolleté rising at the back of the neck to a finely pleated standing ruff. The skirt, falling from the empire waistline, had several gauze-like layers. It was full in the back with a demi-train. The hem was edged with a deep frill of valenciennes lace. The small bodice was covered with the same lace and trimmed with seed pearls that her aunt, and her aunt's mother and grandmother before her, had worn on their wedding dresses. She was allowed to use them because her aunt had no daughter, but she would be expected to give them up if one of Jean-Claude's children proved to be a girl. On the nearest shelf were laid out the full-length white kid gloves, the short, lace-edged veil, the white silk slippers trimmed with satin love knots, and the fan Justin had sent her which she would carry under her bridal bouquet of orange blossoms and white roses.

"Such workmanship, so many tiny stitches, *incroyable*," the hairdresser murmured breathlessly, leaning into the armoire to lift the hem of the gown and peer at the handmade lace. "You will be a beauty beyond compare. You will drive your husband mad. Ah, how I envy you," the woman went on rapturously.

Claire thanked her a little shortly, conscious of the pins that held her hair so tightly and the pressing weight of her orange blossom crown. A headache was beginning just behind her eyes and she wanted nothing more than to be alone so that she could bathe her temples with cologne and sit down for a few minutes without having to smile and pretend or think of what must be done next. But no sooner had they gone than Zaza was sent to her, and the bandboxes with their French landscape scenes painted on their wooden sides must be filled and made ready. She had still not been able to sit down for a moment when her aunt returned to her and summarily dismissed her maid.

"What do you think?" she began as soon as the door closed behind the girl. "Justin Leroux has put away his quadroon mistress. He made her a handsome settlement, gave her the deed to the house in which she was staying, and the gaudy yellow carriage and the matched cream-colored pair he had bought for her, and then walked away while she was vowing her revenge to the heavens!"

"You—you must be mistaken," Claire said faintly. That Justin would have a mistress was not too surprising, but the possibility had not crossed her mind and she hardly knew how to answer her aunt, who stood waiting for her reaction.

"I had it straight from the hairdresser. The woman claims to know Belle-Marie—that is the woman's name—well. She has often been called in to do her hair. And this woman, you know, always knows everything. How many times have you heard it said that the hairdressers hear everything that goes on in Nouvelle Orléans? Well, have you nothing to say? Don't you find it gratifying to know he has done this for you?"

"I prefer to believe that it is because he has decided to leave New Orleans. It might have happened in any case."

"Oh? Hasn't it occurred to you that if he wished he could arrange to have his mistress with him on the plantation? He obviously does not wish it. And by all accounts the woman was incredibly stupid. She treated him to a display of despair and hysterics, threatening to kill herself on one hand and vowing revenge on the other. It would be enough to disgust any man. You will do well to remember it."

"I will try," she said with irony, reflecting that it was highly unlikely that she would ever feel so strongly about anyone.

"And for the love of God, Claire, pull yourself out

of this lethargy you have fallen into, or you will
have your uncle and Jean-Claude suspecting your
reluctance to go to the altar!"

"It is my head," she said, "it aches."

"Then you had best lie down or you will be unfit
for the journey tonight, which if I may say so is the
most ill-advised piece of planning I have ever heard
of. I can't think what our friends will say when they
hear that you do not intend to stay here for the
usual five days. To spend your wedding night rack-
eting across the swamps! It is uncivilized, so *bour-
geois*. But then this whole affair is strange beyond
belief. I don't suppose I can cavil at anything your
future husband takes it into his head to do!"

"No," Claire said. "I find I do not care when we
go, if go we must."

"That is fine for you. You don't have to stay here
and answer all the curious questions."

"I would have thought that you had become ex-
pert at that after these last few weeks."

"Yes, I have sworn *grand comme le bras* that you
are blissfully in love, and you are not going to make
a liar of me. Lie down now. Here, let me place this
bolster just so, under your neck. It will protect your
coiffure. It quite reminds me of the neck rests we
used to use when I was a girl to protect the elaborate frizzed, lacquered, and powdered styles we affected. You have never known agony until you have
worn one of those structures of pins and curls, garlands and ribbons and beads for two weeks. They
weighed pounds, I do swear." Having seen Claire
settled, her aunt rang for the maid and stood waiting.

When Zaza appeared she instructed her to pre-

pare a bath, and since Zaza had already heated the
water it was soon done. The maid went to the armoire to lay out the wedding gown, and she had it
in her arms along with the matching chemise and
the underdress, when suddenly, with a scream, she
let the silken garments fall.

"A *gris-gris!*" she babbled. "A *gris-gris!*"

She turned wide, terrified eyes toward them,
pointing with a trembling finger to the bottom of
the armoire.

"What are you talking about, you stupid creature?" Madame de Hauterive demanded, moving
toward the girl. "Pick up that gown at once!"

"Yes, madame, but—but it is a doll of death! For
Mam'zelle Claire!"

Madame de Hauterive hesitated, then leaned into
the armoire and gingerly picked up a scrap of dirty
white material. It was a doll, a rag of stuffed cloth
dressed in a caricature of a wedding gown and veil,
and impaled through the body by a long, sharp
splinter of wood. As she moved it from its resting
place a black ball fell from the rags, landing on the
floor with a dull thump.

Zaza gasped, and, snatching the gown from the
floor near the ball, moved hurriedly away to stand
shivering in the far corner.

"What was that?" Claire asked, sitting up in bed
so that she could see.

"It is the conjure ball, mam'zelle," Zaza whispered. "It—it is of wax—and black—for evil—"

Even Madame de Hauterive had lost a little of
her color. "How did this loathsome thing get in
here?" she asked stridently. "Who dares to strew

my house with this immoral, heathen voodoo magic?"

"The—the woman who was here, the hairdresser," the maid stammered. "It is said that she knows the Voodooienne."

"And she was near the armoire." There was a look of revulsion on the older woman's face.

"But why?" Claire said. "I hardly knew her, and I certainly never harmed her."

"For Belle-Marie, I would imagine. It seems the kind of thing you might expect from her kind. I expect she paid the hairdresser to get it into the house."

"What did she expect to gain? I'm not a servant to be frightened into illness."

"Revenge, I would imagine, was her aim. She must think you are the cause of her displacement. And as for effectiveness, you have felt unwell since she placed this—this thing in your room."

"It is the hairstyle, the tightness!"

"Are you certain?" her aunt asked in a strained voice.

"Yes, of course! It couldn't be anything else." What was the matter with her aunt? Surely she didn't believe in this voodoo cult so favored by their African slaves and the free men and women of color in New Orleans?

"I knew a woman once, a French woman, whose husband took a mistress. She went to a voodoo queen called Sanitè Dèdè who made a *gris-gris* for her to use to keep her husband at home. She carried the woman one of her husband's gloves and Sanitè Dèdè filled it with—oh, I don't know, dust, and bits of bone and sugar. She also gave her powders in paper twists to put in his food. But as impossible as it may seem, the voodoo worked."

"But—"

"Don't scoff, girl. There are strange things that have happened. I could tell you things that you, as a protected *jeune fille*, have never heard of. These people who have been given into our care, the slaves, have ancient ways we cannot understand. I have known maids who went demented, men who had died for no known reason except for the sprinkling of a little dust, the burning of a few candles of a different hue. I don't suppose you will heed me, but what the quadroon has done once can be done again."

Claire felt a pang of disquiet. To have her usually stolid aunt upset by the voodoo *gris-gris* gave it more importance.

"Fetch me a towel," her aunt told Zaza, and when it was brought she picked up the wax conjure ball with it to protect her fingers, then laid the doll on its folds. "I will throw these things in the fire in the kitchen and say a Hail Mary for your safety, as insurance. Try not to think of it. Get some rest, if you can. You have a long evening before you."

But Claire did not try to rest. It would have been impossible. If her thoughts had allowed it, her pounding head and the turmoil in her mind would not. She bathed slowly in the copper tub filled with warm, scented water, and then, though she felt ill with nerves, she let Zaza slip the low-necked chemise over her head, then the underdress of white silk. Finally, the wedding gown itself was settled carefully into place and the ribbon draw-tapes pulled tightly about her rib cage, just under the bust, and tied in the back. Kneeling before her, Zaza rolled gossamer silk stockings up her legs and fastened them above the knee with rose embroidered garters, then placed the white silk slippers on her feet. For jewelry, she wore nothing but the groom's gift of pearl teardrops.

When she had repaired the slight disorder of Claire's coiffure, touched her face with rice paper squares to remove the sheen and whisked red rose petals across her cheekbones, she stepped back and clasped her hands together.

"Ravishing, mam'zelle. Utterly ravishing. If that one, that Belle-Marie, could see you now she would dry up and fly away with the envy!"

Claire stared at herself in the mirror, hoping the glitter in her eyes might be mistaken for sparkle. Then she smiled at the maid. "You deserve the credit, Zaza. You are a genius. I wish I could take you with me, it would be so much more comfortable having someone I know and could talk to near me. But my—fiancé says that he does not wish my uncle to provide me with a maid, he prefers to do so himself."

"Yes, I understand, mam'zelle. You must bow to the wishes of the man you marry, it is expected. But I, too, will miss you." She smiled impishly. "There is no pleasure in dressing madame, your aunt, only a vast challenge!"

Claire could not help laughing, but that small lift of the spirits did not last beyond the door of her room.

The rain had stopped, but the sky was still overcast, making it seem later than just dusk when she entered the first of a long line of carriages waiting outside the door. The others contained the many relatives of her aunt's family, who must, of course, as her relatives-by-marriage, join the procession. With her rode only her aunt and uncle. It was but a few blocks to the cathedral, but it took some time for the dozen or more carriages to pull up before that building, with its two rounded towers, and more time for their occupants to step down. While they were waiting, Justin joined them, standing on the banquette, or sidewalk, talking to her uncle through the carriage window. He was dressed with an elegant simplicity in a gray cut-away coat, white silk cravat, a white- and gray-striped waistcoat, and white doeskin pantaloons over black evening shoes. The light from the lantern hanging under the portico of the cathedral played over his strong features, leaving his scar mercifully in shadow. From the dim interior of the carriage, Claire had murmured a greeting, then clenched her hands together in her lap, wishing that this ordeal was over, that the next twenty-four hours, or even the next week, could magically pass.

At last they were all gathered. Her uncle handed her down and led her toward the heavy double doors of the cathedral. As they drew near, the regular detail of Swiss Guards in their blue, red, and yellow uniforms came to meet them, to lead them in a slow, majestic march up the aisle. Behind Claire came Justin with her aunt on his arm, and following them was the best man, a friend of Justin's whom Claire had never met before and doubted that she would again. He was escorting a spinster sister of her aunt. After them came Jean-Claude with his grandmother, followed by all the other relatives—

cousins, great-aunts, and great-uncles. The procession should have included Justin's relatives also, most particularly his mother and father, but they were unable to attend the wedding, or so he had claimed.

There was a moment of confusion while everyone with the exception of Claire, Justin, and the best man was seated; then with her hand upon his gloved wrist, Justin led Claire toward the altar where the robed priest awaited them. She slipped the ribbon of her bridal fan, with her bouquet attached, over her left wrist, and she and Justin knelt.

The Church did not permit the celebration of Mass after noon, and so the ceremony was brief. The sonorous words rolled over her head, the ring was slipped onto her trembling finger, and in a few short moments she found herself with a quill in her hand signing the cathedral register, with Justin at her side and all the relatives who had accompanied them waiting behind her to sign also.

It was dark when they passed through the great double doors again. A curious crowd had gathered and a ragged cheer went up as they appeared. Beside her, Justin lifted his hand in acknowledgment, then he checked himself, exclaiming impatiently under his breath.

Following the direction of his gaze, Claire saw a small curricle pulled up near the corner of Chartres Street. In the light of a street lamp slung diagonally across the street on a rope she could see that the carriage was painted a brilliant yellow with orange trim. In it was a woman, for the flash of jewels caught the light of the oil lantern. The thong of a

carriage whip was a sudden blur in the air, then
the matched pair of cream horses surged forward.
The curricle swung wide to turn toward the levee,
then disappeared, hidden by branches of the syca-
more trees that grew in double file in the Place
D'Armes fronting the cathedral.

Belle-Marie. Justin's mistress had come to see
him wed. Claire felt a faint stir of anger. Such effrontery. The woman must know that her carriage
was unmistakable. Did she hope to spoil their wedding day by showing herself, hoping to be a painful
reminder of a secret part of Justin's past life? If
that was her motive, then she was wasting her
venom, Claire thought. Nothing could possibly
make this day more grim than it was already. Or
perhaps her presence was aimed at Justin alone; a
reminder of what he was throwing away?

She glanced up at Justin, but his face was a mask,
devoid of expression.

People began to press around them as the others
left the church. As if only at that moment aware
that he was standing still, he looked at her, then
led her swiftly toward the carriage, handed her in,
and climbed in beside her.

There were more than a hundred guests at the
reception to partake of the champagne and the lav-
ish supper arranged by Madame de Hauterive. No
one was going to be able to say that she had stinted
on the wedding of her husband's ward and niece.
The large salon, and also the small one reserved
usually for the family, had been thrown together.
Tables had been set up along one wall to hold the
food, and the guests milled around them exclaiming at the bounty, the *bouillabaisse* and *court bouil-*

lon, the *daube glacé*, the *vol-au-vents* filled with snipes tongues, and the sweets, the *tartes aux pêches*, the wine and jelly cake, the bride's cake, of course, and the *pièce monteé*—centerpiece—of nougat molded in the shape of the cathedral.

Claire and Justin, after being presented formally, mingled with the guests, ate a little of the supper spread out around them, then with Justin standing impatient at her side, Claire cut her cake and parceled it out among the unmarried girls who promptly wrapped it in a napkin. Each one would sleep with it under her pillow and hope to dream of her future husband.

With that last ceremonious act, Claire slipped away, and with Zaza's aid, changed into a carriage dress of rose cambric with a narrow skirt that would not crush easily. Draping an India shawl over her arms, she waited while Zaza packed her wedding gown and accessories into a dress box. As she stood there, her gaze went to the bed and she reflected that if she had married anyone other than Justin she would now be dressed in her nightgown and negligee with her hair brushed about her shoulders, sitting up in that bed awaiting her husband. With that thought in mind it did not seem such a terrible thing to be starting out on an all-night journey, even if her destination was a strange house called Sans Songe, a house without illusions.

Chapter Three

Zaza handed the dress box to the liveried coachman, bade Claire a good journey, wished her happiness, then hurried back into the house hiding her tears. The driver stowed the box away in the covered luggage rack of the traveling coach, a diligence built for speed. In the light of the coach lanterns, Claire could see a groom, also in livery, at the heads of the four black horses before the coach to hold them, for they were nervous from being kept standing. At the rear of the coach a saddle horse was tied, and she supposed him to be a favorite mount Justin was taking with him into the country.

She turned back to embrace her uncle and aunt standing in the doorway to see the couple off, and bid them farewell. And she pressed her bridal bouquet into her aunt's hand, asking her one last favor: to send it to her convent school, as was the custom. Then swallowing on the constriction of

42

tears that had suddenly arisen in her throat, she turned toward the man waiting for her, his tall form indistinct in the darkness.

"Come," he said, holding out his hand, and there was nothing she could do but obey.

The carriage bowled along the muddy streets at a fast pace, quickly leaving the city behind. As they passed the last of the straggling shotgun houses beyond Rampart Street heading west, they heard the nine o'clock curfew gun in Congo Square boom out. For a few miles, several horsemen, members of the wedding party, followed them singing and shouting, but they soon fell back.

They traveled through the night silence, and as they rode hour upon hour without speaking, some of the tension began to leave her. It was a dark night. Clouds hid the moon, and the side lanterns threw only the faintest glimmer of light inside the coach. She could see the white sheen of Justin's cravat and pantaloons, his outline against the window, but he was so still and seemingly lost in thought that after a time her painful awareness of his presence beside her began to fade.

Claire leaned back in her corner of the diligence. The upholstery was soft velvet, dark blue, like the body of the coach, and luxuriously padded. She rested her head against the squabs, conscious of how weary she was, and of the dull ache that still lived in her head despite the champagne she had drunk. She stripped off her gloves and put her fingers to her eyes, then heedless of the damage to her coiffure she began to remove the heavy crown of orange blossoms that she still wore. There was a slight rustle beside her and something warm touched her hands. She flinched away.

"Allow me to help you." Justin's voice was warm and low, close to her ear.

"N-no, I can manage," Claire said, drawing away from him and tearing the flowers from her hair in her haste.

"Take your hair down also, if you like. It will be a long night, and you might as well be comfortable. There is still quite a distance ahead of us."

"Thank you, no."

"Why not? You should not mind that I will see you. You are, after all, my wife."

It was as if, feeling her draw away from his touch a few seconds before, he had deliberately chosen to remind her of her position.

"I am not likely to forget it," she flared. "But I do not wish to arrive at your home with my hair down around my waist."

"It will be nearly the break of day before we arrive at Sans Songe, and I can assure you that it is not in the least likely that anyone will be up to see you. That is a long time to be uncomfortable, but you could put it back up again if being untidy bothers you."

"Not," she said distinctly, "without my personal maid."

"That rankles? I regret that you are disturbed, but I found myself unable to bear the thought of accepting your uncle and aunt's reluctant charity when there are more than enough women at Sans Songe to attend to your needs. But for the moment you will have to accept my services—as distasteful as they may be."

Without waiting for her assent he began to remove the pins from her hair and toss them into her lap. To avoid prolonging the moment of intimacy longer than need be, Claire helped him. The chignon started to slip, then the heavy coil slid down her shoulder to lie upon her breast like a length of ancient gold satin, shimmering with the movement of the carriage. Claire sighed and closed her eyes, then as she felt a light touch, opened them wide again.

Justin had picked up a strand of her hair. He was playing with it, watching the soft curl cling to his fingers. "You were very beautiful this evening. Regal, that is the word that came to me."

"Th-thank you," Claire acknowledged the compliment, her heart beating unevenly as she sensed the gathering purpose behind the calm demeanor. She avoided his eyes, staring out the window, watching the trees that lined the road, black slashes against the gray-black night, whirling past.

"I was proud of you, of the way you looked, the manner in which you held your head high. You have courage. It is an attribute I admire above all others. We have not started out well together, you and I, but perhaps now that we are man and wife it will be possible to begin anew, to shape the eternity that stretches before us to suit ourselves. Have you the courage for that?"

She could not answer. She felt cornered, harassed beyond endurance, and she was not helped by the clamor of the emotional side of her nature, that part of her that had responded to him twice before. She found herself twisting the rings on her finger, the betrothal ring and the ring of alliance that had been placed upon it in the cathedral—the interlocking double ring engraved with the date, her initials, and those of Justin, her husband.

His fingers touched her chin and turned her face toward him. His eyes were hidden in the darkness above her, and yet she could feel their magnetism. Alarm surged through her and she closed her eyes to blot out the sight of him.

"Can you find it within yourself to forget what has gone before and begin again, here? Now?" His voice was husky, and then his lips trailed flame across her eyelids, down her cheeks to the corner of her mouth. His fingers were warm and vibrant as they moved down her neck and beneath her hair, tilting her mouth to receive the growing passion of his kiss.

"No!"

She twisted her head away, striking out, trying to break free of the paralyzing gentleness of his embrace. Her hand caught the side of his face in a sharp blow, and then her wrists were caught in a bruising grip and jerked down.

"No," she said again fiercely, though she lowered her voice for fear the coachman and the groom on the box above them would hear. That single syllable was both an answer to his question and a denial of his caresses.

"Think carefully before you decide," he grated. "I won't ask you again." But she was too incensed to listen to the warning.

"How can I make a pact with you, a man who threatened to murder my cousin if I did not obey your wishes? What kind of man are you to expect me to fall in with your—your—"

"Amorous inclinations?"

"—your plans, and meekly agree to make you a comfortable and accommodating wife?" Her voice shook with the strain of putting her resentment into words and also her fear of what he would do to her, but she was determined.

"I agreed to marry you, and I have done so, but I agreed to nothing else. Nothing!"

"You surprise me," he murmured, and she could hear the amusement in his voice. "Why else do you suppose I married you?"

"For—for revenge. You could not bear to let me go unpunished for daring to pity you for having a mutilated face!" She regretted the words as soon as they were out, but there was no calling them back.

His fingers bit into her wrist so that she had to clench her fingers against the sudden pain, but his voice was as smooth as before. "Oh, yes, I had almost forgotten. But long moments before I heard you say those fatal words I had seen you, and wanted you. I saw your hair, *ma petite blonde*, like honeyed silk, and I wanted to bury my fingers in it; the depths of your eyes, such a clear, pure, brown fascinated me, and your skin so white with a hint of wild rose beneath the surface, so different from the sallow crones around you; I wanted to press my lips to it—like this."

His words ended in a whisper as his warm mouth found the pulse beating frantically in her throat. He forced her back against the cushions, and though she fought him, her efforts were feeble against his greater strength. She was crushed beneath him, unable to move as his lips traced the line of her temple, the curve of her cheek, brushed the fine curls before her ears, and then closed over her mouth, moulding it to his hard demand. Her senses blurred, her rage receded, her futile struggles grew weaker until she lay passive in his arms.

At last he raised his head, but it was a moment before she could speak. "I should have known you could not be depended upon to act the gentleman."

"So you should, considering the circumstances," he countered grimly. "But what does playing the gentleman have to do with what is between a man and a woman—especially when that woman is his wife?"

"And now—now you have proven that you can force me to your will, that you care nothing for my feelings. I wish you pleasure then of your reluctant bride." Her voice was hard with the promise that, so far as it was in her power, he would gain nothing.

"Thank you, *ma coeur*," he mocked her. "I have always cared more for what I must take than what is too easily given."

Once again his lips descended. It was several minutes before he released her with a low, satisfied laugh. Reaching above them to a sliding panel set into the front of the coach, he pushed it back and gave the order to stop. As the brakes were applied and they ground to a jolting halt, Justin picked up her hand and put it to his lips.

"I am sure you will be desolate," he said with a touch of gaiety, "but I feel it will be best if I ride the rest of the way. You are much too tempting. I suggest that you try to sleep, while you can."

Catching up his caped great-coat and hat, a *chapeau bras*, that were lying on the opposite seat, he stepped down from the coach. The groom brought his horse forward and he mounted with the smooth ease of one who spends long hours in the saddle. He pulled on a pair of gloves that he took from his coat pocket, quieting his restive mount with a few soft words, then he touched the brim of his hat to Claire, and with a sardonic smile rode away.

Claire pulled her India shawl around her, wrapping the folds more closely for comfort. She was suddenly chilled, and though she was glad to be relieved of Justin's presence, still she had a contrary feeling of being deserted.

While they were stopped, they tarried long enough to rest the horses, then the journey resumed. The coach rocked on through the night, the country grew wilder, the road rougher, and the settlements where all the houses were dark and only the dogs awoke to speed their passing were farther and farther apart. At one lonely plantation they stopped and roused the stable to effect a change of horses. Claire was given a hot drink and was able to stretch her legs before they went on. It was with a certain amount of satisfaction that she felt herself growing sleepy; it seemed to prove how little disturbed she was by her long, emotion-torn day. Slipping off her shoes, she put her feet up on the velvet softness and closed her eyes.

The rumble of thunder woke her. Lightning forked the sky and a wet wind filled with rain struck the coach. Claire shivered and felt a stir of pity for the driver and groom riding up on top. She hoped that they had brought oilskins with them. And where was Justin? His great-coat would hold the rain off for a time, but he would eventually be soaked. Hard on that thought came the fear that he might ride back to join her inside the coach, and hurriedly she pushed her feet into her shoes. Then, gathering her hairpins from the floor and the seat, she smoothed her hair and coiled it in a flat knot on top of her head.

Straightening in her seat, she looked out the window. On one side was the forest, thick, dark and impenetrable, but on the other was a fairly large bayou, its current swollen with the spring rains. It must be near daylight, she realized, for although it was raining she could still see the water running swiftly along and also the thick, green grass studded with wild flowers at the edge of the roadside.

Abruptly the coach tilted forward, and by leaning against the glass she could see that they were heading down to what appeared to be a crossing; a crude, railingless bridge over the bayou. The body of the coach jounced on its springs as the wheels struck the thick hewn planks, then there was a rumbling as they started across. Claire could feel the bridge sag with the weight of the diligence, and her breath caught in her throat, but then they were past the dangerous half-way point and she began to relax.

At that moment she heard a hoarse yell above her. The coach stopped, and began to rock violently as the sounds of scrabbling hooves and frantic neighing came to her. The coach backed, then slewed sideways. A whip cracked and the groom added his voice to the driver's as they encouraged the horses, but the animals seemed to be going mad between the shafts. The coach surged forward, stopped, bucking on its springs, and began to back again. Then there was a sickening drop as the back wheel beneath Claire left the narrow span!

She had to get out. She lunged for the door handle on the opposite side. But as the coach skidded, scraping on its back axle, she missed it. She tried again, and caught it. Clinging to it, she wrenched at it. The other wheel, on the front, went off. For a long moment the heavy diligence balanced, swaying, then slowly it began to topple. Once again, Claire pushed at the handle, and the door swung wide.

She caught at the frame, bracing herself, then she jumped. Even as she left it, she felt the coach gathering speed for the crash into the bayou, saw from the corner of her eye the tangle of screaming horses, and the last desperate effort of the driver standing in the box wrenching at the lines. Then she was falling. There was a rending pain in her chest, and after that, darkness. But just on the verge of unconsciousness, a picture flashed across her mind of one other thing she had seen in that second of jumping. A man on horseback under the trees on the far bank, a man draped in the folds of a caped coat.

There was a wailing, moaning sound in her head, rising and falling, rising and falling. Breathing was difficult. There was a tightness around her chest. She was aware of pain hovering near her, and at the back of her mind terror lingered. She moved her head and the pain came closer.

There was a rustle near her side. "Drink," a brisk voice said. A firm support was slipped under her shoulders and she was lifted. A woman's face was close to hers, not young, not old; neither pretty nor ugly, but square-jawed and strong. Her black hair, sprinkled with gray, was cut like a man's, waving back from her face and over her ears, and Claire stared at it wonderingly, but without too great a curiosity.

Claire drank, and was placed once more against soft pillows. The woman moved out of her line of vision.

She was lying in a great wide bed, she saw, with four soaring posts rising above her to a tester, a *ciel-de-lit* of blue silk shirred toward the center where it was held by a golden sunburst, and caught up at the four corners just above the bedposts by sightless bronze cupids carrying garlands of pink ribbon. From the tester hung bed curtains of blue silk and a white muslin mosquito *baire* secured by blue silk-tiebacks. Memory washed over her in a chilling wave as she stared up at the *ciel-de-lit* of the kind made especially for brides.

"Where am I?" she asked, turning toward the woman who was just setting an empty glass down on a marble-topped commode table against one wall.

"At Sans Songe."

"The coach—it was falling off the bridge. I tried—to jump." Her voice sounded weak, even to her own ears.

"Yes, and you very nearly succeeded. You struck something, the side of the bridge probably. You have one cracked rib and at least two more that have suffered damage."

"I—see."

"Our groom, Sylvest, who was with you, dragged

you from the water. You might have drowned otherwise, for you were unconscious, or so he says."

"I—don't remember." Her head had begun to ache and slowly, carefully, she raised her arm and put her hand to her temple. She could still hear that wailing sound, like a dirge. It had not been a part of some nightmare. She glanced toward the window where white muslin curtains, beneath tasselated, gold velvet over drapes, billowed gently in the breeze coming into the room.

"I—hear—"

"That sound is our people in the quarters behind the house mourning for the driver of your coach. He was killed as he was dragged with the horses from the bridge by the weight of the diligence. He had jumped down among the animals trying to slash the harness and set them free. It was a futile gesture, of course. He lost his life and the horses that did not drown had to be destroyed. It was a most unfortunate incident and I regret that it had to mar your homecoming to Sans Songe."

"So do I," Claire said, "and I am sorry—about the driver. He—behaved well." She moved her hand down over her chest, discovering layers of material wrapped securely about her beneath her gown.

"Bandages," the woman informed her, and as if understanding her puzzlement, went on. "You must stay tightly trussed up, almost corseted for some time, until your ribs heal, I am afraid."

"You—did you do this for me?"

"I am a fairly competent doctor; I have had to be. We are so far from town here. And when an emergency arises one cannot wait a day, the time it takes to send someone for the nearest doctor, one must act."

"I must thank you, Madame—"

"I am only Justin's aunt, his father's sister. You may call me Octavia."

"I am in your debt, Octavia," Claire said simply.

"Think nothing of it. I would have done the same for anyone." She smiled, showing even white teeth.

Claire's gaze was caught by a flash of gold on the side of Octavia's face, and she saw that the woman had gold coins strung on gold wires in her ears. For the first time she noticed also that Octavia wore not the simple pastel empire gown that was the mode, but a strange garment almost like a dressing gown but not constructed like any dressing gown Claire had ever seen. It appeared to be a single piece of wide silk with an opening cut from the head, and holes left on the sides for her arms. Crisp gold braid outlined the armholes, neck, and hem and it was slashed with broad stripes of vivid color; orange, black, green, and gold. On her feet she wore turkish slippers in a violently clashing red velvet, and from her upturned toes dangled small gold tassels.

"Do you like my costume?" Octavia raised her arms to her shoulders causing the sides to flare in great wings. "It is immensely comfortable, to me a greater recommendation than modishness. And, *Bon Dieu!*, who cares to be modish out here in the country? For days on end one never sees company. It is eccentric, yes, but I like that. What else is left for a spinster? I am a mere pensioner living on the favor of my relatives. I make myself useful, but, one must amuse oneself, *n'est-ce pas?* What better than to look into the mirror and see a drollery rather than a hag? Those so delicate, so feminine muslins I am sure you wear with such grace, they are not appropriate for middle-aged ladies of my style. In them I appear grotesque! It is not to be borne. But you must rest instead of listening to my chatter. I will leave you now."

"But wait!" Claire said. "What—what of—"

"What of your husband?" Octavia would not allow her to finish a sentence. "Justin will come later, never fear."

"I thought I—"

"Do not distress yourself unnecessarily. I assure you your husband is as devastated by the accident as you could wish. He has sent for the doctor and eventually one will come, but in the meantime I will cosset you with *tisanes* and by the time he arrives I will have made you nearly well except for the cracked bones. You will see." And with a brief but wide smile Octavia left the room, closing the door behind her.

Claire had intended to tell Octavia that she thought she had seen Justin before she jumped, but perhaps it was just as well that she had been prevented. The woman was his aunt and must be prejudiced in his favor. There was without doubt some form of medication in the drink that Octavia had given her, for in a short while Claire found the room receding in a nebulous mist. The sound of mourning grew farther and farther away, and without knowing precisely when it happened, she fell asleep.

The room was in darkness when she awoke. She was fully alert this time; some strange awareness had cut through the last wisps of drugged sleep like

a knife. The weather had cleared, for beyond the
curtains at the window a full moon shone, drown-
ing the earth in its clear white light. It shed a faint
glow into the room, and in it Claire could see the
door into her bedroom beyond the foot of her bed
slowly open. There was a whisper of sound, then a
waiting quiet. Claire felt the hair on her scalp
prickle, then the bed was jarred and a small black
form appeared at her feet! She stiffened, caught by
pain as she tried to wrench away, then she went
limp, laughing weakly at herself.

It was a cat. Sinuously it began to pick its way
toward her, its feet silent on the coverlet. In its
effortless feline grace there seemed to be an odd
familiarity, and then she shifted in irritation as she
realized that the cat reminded her to Justin—

As it felt her move the cat stopped, on its guard,
aware, perhaps, of her strong antagonism. The
moonlight glistened in its eyes giving it a baleful
menace. It was dark as the night with no relieving
touch of white, a witch's cat, personifying evil. It
had one paw resting on her thigh beneath the cover,
and abruptly it flexed its claws, digging into her
flesh. She bit her lip, brushed by a primeval fright,
and it seemed to her over-imaginative brain that
here was another creature, kin in spirit to Justin,
determined to impose its will on her.

She did not move, she did not even flinch from
the hurt. Slowly there burgeoned inside her a re-
solve not to be intimidated. Anger seeped into her
mind, not against the cat but against Justin and
the situation in which she found herself, and her
own acquiescence that had brought her to lie beneath a bridal blue *ciel-de-lit* against her will.

She stared at the cat with a cold superiority in her eyes. Strength, mental strength, was the solution. She could not be frightened into subjection so long as her will was strong.

For long seconds the cat's eyes met hers, and then he looked away. He glanced back uncertainly, but at last he turned and leaped from the bed, and with his tail low, streaked from the room.

Claire leaned back against the pillows, exhausted by the effort of will, then a wry smile twisted her mouth. What a fool she was to waste so much energy terrorizing a house cat, taking her enmity out on a harmless creature that reminded her of her husband because she did not quite dare release it upon Justin himself.

The room she was lying in was a large one she discovered, looking around her, trying to forget what had just taken place. To her left was a fireplace flanked on each side by large mahogany armoires. To her right was the window, actually a pair of french doors, opening out, she was sure, onto a gallery if Sans Songe was like most houses in Louisiana. Directly before her was another door, the one through which the cat had entered. A pair of slipper chairs in gold velvet and mahogany sat in one corner with a small table holding a whale oil lamp between them. On the wall near the bed was the commode table with a bowl and pitcher in a floral patterned white china upon it. Near the bowl and pitcher sat a small vanity-shaving mirror suspended in a rosewood frame so that it could be tilted, and next to it was a candle in a pewter holder. At the foot of the four-poster on which she lay, she could just discern a day bed of the kind used during the afternoons to avoid marring the smoothness of the feather mattresses. The beds were also known as accouchement beds, for it was upon them that children were born rather than on the awkwardly wide, high, tester bed.

Claire dragged her eyes away from that disturbing piece of furniture, surveying the double armoires, the paired slipper chairs and the vanity-shaving mirror, recognizing with a faint sinking feeling that this was a room furnished for two, a man and his wife.

A light wind caused the curtains at the french doors to waver and Claire realized that they were open. She looked at them with interest, happy to have something else to occupy her mind. In New Orleans her aunt had never allowed the windows to stand open at night. The noxious vapors in the evening air were known to be poisonous, and her aunt had had a great horror of breathing them in her sleep. Should the doors be shut? She could not decide. That faint breeze against her face was very pleasant, scented with the sweet smell of warm grass, magnolias and sweet olive, and bringing to her the night chorus of peeper frogs and crickets and the pleading cry of a night bird.

It brought also the sound of voices out on the gallery, and as she heard them Claire realized that it could not be as late as she had supposed, perhaps not even time for supper. Dinner, at two o'clock, was so late in the day that often supper was postponed until eight or nine. Added to the evidence of the voices was the fact that the mosquito *baire* had not been pulled about her bed. Surely they would not let her sleep for the night without offering her some kind of nourishment and providing protection against the marauding mosquitos?

Then, as she heard her name spoken outside her room, such considerations left her.

"Your Claire is resting comfortably," she heard a cool, languid voice say. "You haven't asked, but I am sure you must want to know."

"Thank you, *maman*." It was Justin who answered in a neutral voice.

"She is a pretty child. I peeped in on her a few hours ago while she slept. One wonders what attracted her to you." There was a destructive undercurrent of old venom in the voice of the woman Justin had called *maman*—mother. Claire frowned in the darkness wondering why a woman would want to hurt her own child by referring in that oblique way to his appearance.

"It was my *beaux yeux*, I don't doubt," Justin answered, "Or my polished address." The irony of that was lost on his mother but not on Claire.

"I am familiar with your address, my son, and I can't agree."

Justin did not appear to be inclined to parry that thrust. He did not speak. And after a moment the woman went on. "But come, I have been waiting all day to discover the cause of this accident. You needn't pretend you don't know, for I am aware that you have been holding a conclave in the quarters the best part of the afternoon. What does Sylvest have to say?"

"Nothing. Nothing at all. He claims that he jumped before he could see what made the horses go wild, and that the thing happened so fast he doesn't really know what took place."

"And you believe that?" It was obvious that his mother did not.

"I wasn't completely satisfied, no. I spoke to one or two of the others who know him well, one of the men he works with and his sister who helps out in the kitchen. It seems that they believe that he is afraid to speak."

"I wonder why?" It was said with a scathing intonation.

"You think it is for fear of me? You are mistaken," he said grimly.

"I, mistaken? I believe that you underestimate the reputation of your temper. But to return to your Claire, you have not been near her room today. I must caution you against neglecting her. Women will stand for much, but never that."

"And you, *maman*," he said softly, "should know well what, and how much, a woman will bear before she turns elsewhere."

"You cannot argue that I always came second with your father, after his plantation, and after you, my son."

"What," he mocked, "aren't you going to throw his mistress into my face this time?"

"Well, can you deny that he had one?" she answered stridently.

"You know I never bother to defend my father to you."

"That poor helpless hulk? I cannot say I like you for that."

"Ah, no, *maman*. But then you cannot say that you like me, can you?"

There was a rustle of skirts as though his mother swung violently away from him, then the sound of footsteps receding. Stillness. The curtains at the french windows swayed and a dark figure stepped into the room; Justin by the shape of his head and the width of his shoulders. He moved noiselessly over the reed matting on the floor. At the foot of the bed he halted, and lifting one clenched fist, he slammed it against the tall post that held the tester in place. But whether the emotion that caused the action was rage or despair, Claire could not have said.

At last he raised his head, and, resting it on his wrist against the bed post, stared in her direction through the darkness. By the time he seemed to be aware of where he was, Claire had shut her eyes and was trying to regulate her breathing, pretending to be asleep. The hush weighed upon her. She heard a faint sound above her and stiffened before she recognized the sliding noise of the mosquito *baire* being drawn about her bed. And seconds later she heard the click of the latch as Justin, leaving the room, closed the door behind him.

Chapter Four

Claire sat in bed, carefully propped up with pillows, with a negligee about her shoulders. It was one of her own, of white batiste, beautifully embroidered in pink, blue, and green by the nuns at the convent which she had attended. A Negro maid, a silent, unsmiling creature called Rachel who had been brought from the parlor to be her serving woman, was brushing her hair carefully and slowly to bring out the sheen.

Sipping a cup of *café noir*, black coffee, Claire watched broodingly as Justin, in front of the mirror, used a pair of silver-backed military brushes on his hair. Over his shoulder he was telling his valet, who was standing before the open doors of one of the great armoires, which coat to lay out for him to wear. In the other matching armoire, Claire's own clothes reposed, rescued from the bayou and meticulously washed and pressed. Many of her things, her wedding gown, her straw bonnets, her velvet hat with its dancing plumes, had been ruined beyond repair, but she did not regret their loss and there had been enough left for her use.

At the foot of her bed was the day bed, its covers dragging onto the floor, where Justin had slept so that he would not injure her accidentally as he turned in his sleep at night. Her gaze traveled to the tray resting on the foot of her bed and littered with the crumbs from breakfast, then to Justin's shaving water, beginning to cool in the china bowl and the linen towels crumpled beside it. For nearly a week, Claire had been a spectator to this morning ritual of breakfast—which she shared—then shaving and dressing. If she lived to be an old woman she would never become used to it.

Justin moved slightly to one side, and she knew he had been watching her face in the mirror when he tossed the brushes to the top of the table and turned to face her. With a brief gesture, he dismissed her maid, then shrugged into the coat his valet held ready before dismissing him also.

"Well, *mon ange*," he said, a glint of laughter in his eyes. "How do you like your married life so far?"

So he had noticed her embarrassment and it had amused him. It did not matter that he was always up and dressed before she awoke. He still managed to suffuse the proceedings of his toilette before her with an air of casually accepted intimacy. Or was it only in her mind? She did not know.

"Have you nothing to say?" he insisted.

"I—I have no objection," she answered, staring into her cup of coffee so black it gave back her reflection.

"Not even to our living arrangement?" He reached out and took the coffee cup from her hand and placed it on the tray.

"It is your room," she said stiffly, avoiding his eyes.

"Our room," he corrected, then went on. "But tell me, how do you feel this morning?"

"Very well. I would like to get up today and go outside, now that the five days are over."

For five days, six counting the day of her arrival that she had spent in drugged sleep, she had been confined to this one room. It was not just her injury, it was also the custom that decreed that a bride and groom must spend the first five days after their wedding in confinement together. Justin, under the circumstances, had not observed the custom strictly, but he had spent much of his time with her. Their meals were brought to them on trays, they had received no one, not even the family, after that first day. They had played backgammon, read, and sometimes she had sketched amusing little flower portraits with pen and ink, as she had been taught, while Justin worked on the plantation accounts, propping the great journals in his lap while he sat in one of the low slipper chairs made for putting on slippers, shoes, and boots, not for comfortable resting. Often they talked—skirting gingerly around anything that bordered on the personal—and in the afternoons they napped, he on the day bed and she alone on the great four poster that reminded her of a catafalque. But in the early morning and late afternoon he left her while he rode out visiting the fields, searching for a breath of air, or so he said. Claire wondered if he enjoyed the reprieve from her company as much as she enjoyed relaxing away from his. Only the doctor, a tall, middle-aged, gangling man with limp fingers and an ingratiating manner, had been allowed to disturb them. He agreed with Octavia's diagnosis, ate an enormous supper, spent the night, and left early the next morning with his fee in his pocket.

"If you will wait until after dinner, I will carry you out onto the back gallery," Justin answered her.

"I'm sure I can manage. I am not nearly the invalid you all make of me."

"I wouldn't dream of allowing you to put your feet to the floor," he said shaking his head, a curl of amusement at the corner of his mouth. "I will give orders that you are not to move until I return."

"Will you?" she countered. "Then I will wait until everyone's back is turned."

"I can see I will have to tie you to the bedposts," he said with a mock sigh.

"You wouldn't!"

"No? I promise you I would. Gently, of course."

"Oh, very well," she agreed, looking away, willing the flush on her cheeks to subside.

"Come, Claire," he said softly, his eyes on her gold-tipped lashes. "You can't begrudge me this small victory. These past few days have been yours."

She raised startled eyes to his. "I don't know what you mean."

"I think you do. Underneath your injured ribs you must be laughing inside. You won."

"What?"

"You agreed to 'nothing else—' " he quoted.

Comprehension came, and with it, confusion. There was a grain of truth in what he implied. She had welcomed the injuries of her accident, since it prevented the consummation of their marriage. But to say so would sound like a challenge she knew only too well he would answer with all speed. And yet, to deny the accusation would be to invite his embrace.

He laughed, a low sound that had a hollow ring, and reached out to lift her chin so he could look into her eyes. "Don't panic. I am not forcing you to the wall. I find, to tell you the truth, that I have enjoyed our days together. I enjoyed your smiles that were neither afraid nor—designed to delude others into thinking you were deliriously happy. They were friendly smiles, I think, unaffected, without guile—for a change."

Claire wished, as the quiet seconds passed, that she could agree, could say that she too had enjoyed their days together, but the lie stuck in her throat. She had not enjoyed them. She had known constantly that she was only there because Justin willed it. And she had never been certain, given his reputation for ruthlessness, that he would consider a cracked rib and a few bruises a deterrent to his desires. His presence, regardless of what he was doing, made her nervous, less perhaps in the last day or two, but still she was certain she would never be able to ignore his presence as he so easily could her own.

A look of cynicism came into his eyes as she remained silent. "I am a fool. But I find I prefer a smile in your eyes to hate or fear. And so I will wait—for as long as my short patience will allow. In the meantime I would advise you to take great care. Your best protection will be in total indifference, or in a consistent expression of distaste, for I warn you, I intend to take advantage of your first moment of weakness."

She drew in her breath sharply, but before she could turn her head he dropped a kiss upon her parted lips. Then he got to his feet and, picking up his hat from the table beside the bed, stepped through the open french window out onto the gallery. She was so bemused she did not hear him walk away.

Rousing herself from her reverie, Claire picked up the small silver bell from the table beside her bed and rang for Rachel. She knew her maid would be waiting not far away. As she gave the order for her bath to be prepared, she heard a louder bell. It was one of several hanging on the small enclosed gallery, or loggia, in the back. Her room, she had discovered, was off by itself at the rear of the house, flanked on either side by galleries. According to Justin, the house was of the French planter style perfected in the West Indies. It was built in a great square of nine rooms, three wide and three deep, surrounded on three sides by galleries to shade and protect the house from the sun and rain. Built up on tall, massive brick pillars in the manner known as a raised basement, its lower floor was used for storage only, since in the spring it was subject to flooding from the bayou that looped and curved around the plantation. The raised basement gave the house the look of two stories, a look enhanced by the hipped roof pierced by dormers. The main floor was the only one used by the family, and was reached by sweeping staircases, front and back, leading from the ground to the second floor.

In the center front of the house, directly before the stairs, was the salon which opened by high, wide double doors into the dining room, which in turn gave onto the back loggia. On each side of these rooms ran the bedrooms, each opening out onto the gallery and often into the rooms next to them, so that during the hottest weather the entire house could be thrown open to the free circulation of the slightest breeze.

Claire's room, at the back of the house, had a greater privacy than most. Though it had access to the side gallery, there was none to the back loggia and the one other door which gave into Octavia's bedroom was fixed with a large and efficient silver-plated lock.

In her own room, there was a bell pull that rang one of the different toned bells outside. Justin used it often to summon his valet or for a servant to bring a meal, a hot bath, or simply a boy to carry messages for him. But since the pull was located beside the fireplace, Claire could not reach it from where she lay. The bell that had rung, she thought, was for the personal maid of Justin's mother. Helene, the mistress of the house, must be about to rise.

In the days that she had lain in bed she had come to recognize the different bell notes and the members of the family to whose rooms they were connected. Sounds had a way of echoing through the house. She had learned that Justin's mother was a demanding mistress, constantly requiring something. She had learned, too, that across the back loggia from her own room was the room of Justin's father who was an invalid—though the servants were slow to answer his bell, perhaps because it was rung not by him but by his manservant. She knew that there was another woman in the house, Berthe Leroux, Justin's aunt. Claire suspected that Berthe was the widow of Justin's uncle, the man he had killed. But Justin had not told her anything of the matter.

Berthe Leroux seemed to be a woman of modest requirements, for her bell seldom rang, though apparently she too had her own maid, a shuffling older woman given to muttering beneath her breath. And there was also Berthe's son, Justin's cousin, who had the room beyond Octavia's; a pleasant enough man from what she could tell. He laughed often, sang in his bath, and woke in an ill-humor, for his voice was perfectly audible as he castigated his valet in colorful language in the morning hours.

But though Helene might be mistress of the house in name, Claire had decided that it was Octavia who stood at the center of it. It was she who planned the menus, supervised the maids, spoke to the gardeners and often stepped out on the gallery to meet Justin when he returned from the fields. There they would talk for a time about the crops in the home fields, the kitchen gardens, the orchards of peach, pear, and bushy figs and the animals that must be cared for to provide the bounty that came to the table. And though Octavia, it seemed, should have used her bell often with her many activities, it almost never rang. Claire knew, because of the closeness of their rooms, that the older woman had little

use for a maid, that she bathed and dressed herself,
did her own hair, and was much more likely to go
in search of the servant she wanted than to set her
bell to clamoring.

As she bathed, Claire considered the people who
lived in the house with a rising interest. At last,
today, she would meet them instead of lying in her
bed listening, trying to visualize what they looked
like and how they would accept her. Now that the
five days were over she would be able to receive
visitors as well as be able to leave her room herself.
Would Justin's family resent her? It seemed likely,
for none of them had thought it convenient to attend her wedding and of them all, only Justin's father had been really unable to come to New
Orleans. A wedding celebration was an occasion
that few Creoles cared to miss in the ordinary way,
but these people had ignored the marriage of the
man who was in actuality the head of the house and
the master of the plantation, even if he was not so
in fact. Why else would they have done that unless
they disapproved of the woman he had chosen as
his bride?

Claire was just easing her arms into a fresh peignoir when Octavia swept into the room. "Charming, I'm sure. But I would like to know who gave
you permission to remove your bandages for a bath?
I will have to wrap you up again, you know.
Couldn't you have had Rachel give you a refreshing
rub with eau de cologne? You should not be up. I
am persuaded Justin will not like it."

"What business is it of—" she began, then flushed
as Octavia raised an eyebrow. "But surely it cannot

matter," she protested. "He has said that he will carry me out onto the back gallery this afternoon."

"The man has no more sense than a moonling. You should lie quietly for at least a month."

"Can't I lie quietly outside? I am so very tired of this room."

"An admission you should not make, my dear. All brides should profess to be reluctant to leave their confinement. It is expected."

Claire stared at her, caught by the warning tones in her voice and a trace of sternness. But Octavia avoided her eyes, and, with a competent and domineering air that was faintly annoying, whisked her into bed, where she rebandaged her ribs to a tightness that left her panting but did relieve the pain.

The other woman instructed Rachel in clearing the room, twitched the covers into place, handed her a book, one of Mrs. Radcliffe's romances translated into the French, then paused in the act of leaving.

"I didn't come to nursemaid you, though I am happy to do so. I came to warn you to expect a visit from Helene, and possibly, if she can screw up the courage, Berthe."

"Oh?"

"By all rights your husband should have conducted his mother to meet you himself. It would have been much more *comme il faut*. But he will not, and Helene can no longer conquer her curiosity. I overheard her saying to Berthe that a visit of condolence would be a polite gesture and a satisfactory solution under the circumstances, and so I am sure the royal visit is pending."

"I am glad you told me. The prospect is fright-

ening enough without being caught at a disadvan-
tage by surprise."

"Oh, you need not fear Helene or Berthe—" she
hesitated as if considering the wisdom of what she
was about to say, then a resolute expression passed
over her face and she raised her chin. "But perhaps
I should warn you: Justin and his mother are not
on the best of terms. You would do well to take
care. You would not wish, I am sure, to be caught
in the middle of their quarrel. Just remember that
it does not concern you—you need not fear that it
does. It concerns what has happened in the past. It
need not trouble you unless you allow it to or unless you allow yourself to become a pawn in their
battle."

"But I don't understand. Why should they be at
war with one another?"

"You must wait for Justin to tell you. He will, I
imagine, when he is ready for you to know. I cannot
interfere. Put it from your mind. If I were you I
would think well before I asked at all. There is time
enough and more to learn the black heart that lies
at the center of the *fleur de la pois*."

The *fleur de la pois*—the flower of the pea—the
pick of the lot: that had been the name of the plantation before it became Sans Songe. What had Octavia meant? Claire pondered it after the older
woman had gone. She did not know, but it seemed
to be sound advice that the older woman had given
her. She was in no hurry to learn the dark secrets
of her unwanted husband.

Because of the custom of the five days, Claire had
had no visitors to her bedroom. Now that was
changed. True to Octavia's prediction, toward the

middle of the morning there was a knock on the door and before she could call *entrez*, two women stepped into the room.

"I bid you a good morning," the woman in the lead said, and Claire, hearing the slow, rather bored tones, did not need the introduction to know that this was Justin's mother. She was tall for a woman, and painfully thin, with delicate features in a heart-shaped face and enormous, purple-shadowed dark eyes. At one time she might have been a beauty, but now there was a ravaged look about her face. Her hair was fading into gray and her apparently permanent state of tension could be seen in the taut tendons that corded her neck and the backs of her slender hands. But though unhappiness had marked her, she had at least a visible personality. That was more than could be said for the woman in black who trailed into the room behind her.

"My sister-in-law, Berthe. Her husband and mine were brothers. As you can readily see, however, she is a widow—and I am certain that you know that the blame for that state lies at the door of my son."

The woman called Berthe was a colorless nonentity with watery brown eyes surrounded by such pale lashes that she seemed to have none. Her hair was stuffed under a cap of black muslin edged with black ribbon with long streamers hanging down her back. Her high-necked, long-sleeved dress was of black sarsenet with an empire waist and wide skirts over several layers of petticoats that gave her a ludicrous appearance of width, not helped by her tendency toward plumpness.

Her pasty face turned a shade paler as she gasped

in a thin voice, "Helene, you should not say such things, not to your son's bride. It—it is shocking."

"But true, and if she doesn't know it now she is sure to hear it eventually. I find it hard to believe that she could be ignorant of it."

"I—I knew of the unfortunate incident, of course."

"There! I told you. Unpleasant things have a way of coming to our attention."

Searching her mind for a change of topic, Claire bethought herself of the duties of one receiving guests.

"Won't you please sit down, there in the slipper chairs if you could pull them closer? And perhaps you would like a cup of coffee and a few small cakes?"

"That is very kind of you," Helene said, taking her seat, "but you need not trouble yourself. I have only this moment finished my morning coffee and I never indulge in sweets before dinner." She let her eyes flick in the direction of short, plump Berthe.

"No, no, nothing for me," Berthe said hurriedly.

An unpleasant smile touched Helene's mouth, then she raised her eyes and looked around the room. "I hope you are comfortable here, and that you have everything that you desire. If not, you have only to ask and it will be brought to you— within reason, of course. This is a nice room; I have always thought it one of the best in the house. My husband and I used it, you know, when we were first married. It has been close to ten years since I was last in it. Unbelievable, isn't it?"

"The room is—very nice," Claire said, choosing the one thing in what Helene had said with which she could agree.

"And Rachel, she is acceptable?"

"Oh, yes, she is surprisingly well trained, considering that she was a parlor maid and not versed in tending to ladies."

"I am glad she pleases you. I chose her for you myself."

"Th-thank you," Claire said, glad that she had expressed approval of the girl. "I am most grateful. I am sure I don't know what I would have done without her."

Berthe, who had been very quiet, spoke suddenly. "Rachel is a sister to my girl."

"I didn't know. She never speaks of her family."

"Which is as it should be. I cannot abide a chatterer," Helene stated.

Claire, who would have preferred a friendlier personality in her servant, forbore to disagree with her.

"As pleasant as this room may be, I am sure you are becoming weary of it. As soon as you are able to be up and about we must go for a drive in my carriage and show you a little more of our holdings here."

"I would enjoy that. I have grown very curious about the country around the house, and about where Justin goes and what he does when he is away."

"You haven't questioned him about his movements? I see you are beginning to know my son," Helene said with a dry note in her voice.

"Helene—" Berthe protested. But her sister-in-law barely glanced at her.

"And as to where he goes and what he does, *ma*

chère, perhaps I should tell you before someone else does—"

"Helene!"

"Don't bleat, Berthe!"

"But you don't know—"

"With the Leroux men it is not necessary to know, to see with your own eyes. You of all people should understand that, Berthe."

"I beg you—" It was barely a whisper, but in that softly breathed sound there was such anguish that Claire wanted somehow to help that plain woman in the black dress. There was nothing she could do except look away from the pale, trembling lips and the small, lashless eyes that glittered with tears and something else she could not quite define.

"What I wished to inform you of," Helene's emotionless voice went on, "is that my son's quadroon has been seen in the vicinity. I feel personally that it is better in cases like this to be forewarned—and I am not without experience."

Claire stared at her. What could she say? A part of her greeted the news with apathy, but another part felt a shaft of pure jealousy—not, she assured herself, because of any concern for her husband, but for the security of her position as his wife, a position, under their religious beliefs, that she must hold until death.

"Your concern does you credit, I'm sure—" she began, and then stopped as Helene sprang to her feet, her gaze fixed on the cat that had just walked in at the partially open french window from the gallery.

"Put that animal out! I cannot bear cats. How Octavia can stand to have him in her room is more than I will ever understand. I loathe him, sneaking, slinking creature. One never knows where he will be next!"

It was the first time that Claire had seen the great black cat since the night he had frightened her, but now she was grateful for the diversion. She made no move to evict him as he leaped upon her bed and curled himself into a ball.

"There are a great many people who cannot abide cats," she said, smiling a little. "For myself, I like them well enough. They are clean animals, and quiet." She glanced at Berthe and found that lady also staring at the cat, a peculiar expression on her face, half antipathy, half thoughtfulness.

"Please yourself," Helene said tautly. "But don't let him scratch you. I have always heard that cats carry poison in their claws."

The two ladies did not linger much longer, and when the door had closed behind them, Claire reached out and slowly began to scratch between the cat's ears. He stretched, pressing against her hand, and she smiled and smoothed his fur, thinking.

Why had Helene told her about Belle-Marie? What was her purpose? She doubted it was the one given. What was the thing that lay between Helene and her son that caused her to speak of him with such bitterness? Claire was almost certain that her mother-in-law was disappointed in her reaction to her news. Had she expected that Claire would be shocked and hurt, or possibly, jealous? Was that what she had wanted?

Justin did not return to the house for the midday meal, and Claire ate alone except for the great

black cat with whom she shared her dinner. She
had little appetite, and the cat would keep Octavia
and the cook in the kitchen from feeling hurt because she had rejected their carefully planned meal.
Then, while she should have been resting during
the long afternoon, she lay staring at a shadow box
filled with flowers made of human hair that hung
on the opposite wall. Her book, with its improbable
characters and happenings, no longer appealed. The
room was stuffy, her mattress hard, her two pillows
too soft so that the hard roll of the bolster was too
firm beneath her neck. The tightness of the bandage around her chest irritated her and she shifted,
acknowledging with a sigh that her ribs ached.

She missed having someone to talk to, someone
near while she slept, she told herself. That was all.

Still, when Justin stepped through the door she
sat up straighter and summoned a smile. For the
moment she had relegated Belle-Marie to the back
of her mind.

He stood for a moment, letting his eyes become
accustomed to the dark room after the sunlight, and
in that moment of temporary blindness, Claire saw
that he looked tired, with lines of grimness about
his mouth.

"Good afternoon," she said, and then gripped her
hands together as she saw a shadow of annoyance
cross his face. It was much too formal a greeting,
but what would be the correct address to a husband
who was nearly a stranger—and one who might be
coming from his mistress?

"Why aren't you resting?" he asked, walking forward to stand beside the bed.

"I couldn't sleep, and as for resting, I have done nothing else for this week."

"You are ready then, I take it, to get up?"

"If I may," Claire answered, pleating the sheet between her fingers, tinglingly aware of his closeness and the warmth and the fresh smell of the outdoors that emanated from him.

"Did you intend to go like this?" He reached out and touched the embroidery that embellished the sleeve of her peignoir.

"I'll change, of course," she said, sensing a softening in his manner.

"Do so. I am going to see if I can get Cook to reheat something for me for a late dinner. I will send Rachel to you."

Claire nodded, and Justin began to turn away when he stopped and bent down. He picked something up from the floor near the foot of her bed where the bedspread sagged onto the rug. He straightened slowly, staring at the thing he held in his hand, a ball of white chicken feathers with a piece of string dangling from it.

"How did this get in here?" he demanded.

"I don't know, I've never seen it before. What is it?"

"I'm not sure," he said, slowly turning it in his hands, a speculative look on his face.

"It—it's a *gris-gris*—isn't it? Claire said suddenly, the moment the thought occurred. "A *gris-gris* from Belle-Marie, just like the other one."

Chapter Five

"WHAT DO YOU mean, just like the other one?"

As his voice snapped out, she ran her tongue nervously over her lips. "Like the—the one found in my room on our wedding day, a bride made of rags with a splinter—"

"Why wasn't I told?"

"It was our wedding day—" she tried to explain without understanding herself exactly what she meant. "And we were leaving New Orleans and—and all that behind."

His face took on a grim cast. "And what does that mean?"

"Surely you know?" Claire spread her hands helplessly. "My aunt explained to me."

"She told you about my mistress." It was not a question. There was a fatalistic ring in his voice.

"Yes, that is, she told me you had put her aside. So naturally I assumed—"

"You thought you were the target of revenge?"

"It seemed that I must be—that is, who else would have done it? Who else had a reason?"

"It is impossible. She would not dare."

"She must have! She was there at our wedding, staring at me as if she wished me dead. And now she is here."

Claire flinched as he turned his gaze, black with anger, on her. Looking away she found herself staring at the thing in his hand.

"Do you know what this is? What it's for?"

She shook her head.

"It's a death *gris-gris*, and as its counterpart in the hands of the Voodooienne is unwrapped slowly, day by day, it is supposed to cause the cursed one to sicken and die by degrees."

The other *gris-gris*, the doll, had had the splinter of wood through its chest. Claire had been injured in the chest by the wooden bridge. Coincidence or not? Might this new *gris-gris* not be more effective? The shadow of fear clouded her vision.

Justin stared into her wide eyes. "You don't believe in this nonsense?" He crumpled the object in his hand. "It's nothing but mumbo-jumbo directed at the gullible among the Negroes. It can't hurt people like us."

"Can't it?" she asked, wanting to be reassured.

"Not by itself," he said cryptically, and turned away.

"Justin—"

"Yes," he grated, swinging back.

"What are you going to do?"

"Don't press it, Claire. Dismiss it from your mind.

That part of my life, the people I knew before we met, have nothing to do with you."

"I hope you are right," she said, holding his gaze until he turned away.

She dressed in an empire afternoon costume of jonquil muslin with a sleeveless spencer of apple green and slippers of the same color tied with yellow ribbons. Over her arms she slipped her India shawl against the cool breeze that moved the trees gently outside in the bright sun.

When Justin returned, she was standing in the middle of the floor. He scooped her up unceremoniously into his arms and turned toward the outer door.

"My father is taking the sun out on the loggia, too. This is as good a time as any for you to meet him. I may have told you that he is paralyzed, has been since he suffered a stroke years ago. You will do all right if you remember that though he can't speak, he hears very well and his understanding is excellent—at least, I assume so. He manages to communicate simple messages to Anatole, his man. Try not to feel uncomfortable, if you can."

Claire nodded, glad to have this to think of to take her mind from the hard strength of the arms that carried her so effortlessly out onto the gallery, around the front of the house, then back through the salon and dining room to the small semi-enclosed loggia. Compared to the other open galleries that surrounded the house, this was a small area. It was encircled on three sides by the walls of the house, with only the fourth open with a plain bannister railing and four graceful colonnettes fronting it. The back steps led directly from it to the ground. The loggia was furnished with woven-cane chairs and settees and two crude plantation-made rockers with rope seats. Baskets of fern lent cool notes of green to the corners.

Justin settled her on a settee piled with cushions, and she thanked him rather breathlessly before she looked toward the man lying on a cane chaise nearby.

He was an old man with thinning, dull, gray-streaked brown hair, and the colorless complexion of one who has been ill for a long time. There was no expression in his brown eyes, no smile on his face. And though he was dressed with neatness and even a touch of dandyism in the sheen on his new-looking black boots and the gold seals and fobs that hung from the watch pocket of his pantaloons, he was overweight, due perhaps to inactivity. But in contrast to the thickness of his body the skin of his face was stretched over the bones, and on his thin hands, that hung with an almost lifeless stillness from his sleeves, were brown liver spots.

"My dear, may I present my father, Marcel Leroux. And behind him is Anatole, his arms, legs, and tongue."

The pale man on the chaise stared at her. After an interminable time he made a faint movement of his head, and the slim, wiry Negro standing at the head of the chaise spoke softly, "My master and I bow to you, Madame Leroux."

Madame Leroux. It seemed so distant, so formal. She pulled her shawl around her, forcing herself to smile and acknowledge the greeting with a suitable reply.

"What a nice place this is," she continued, gaz-

ing out beyond the flight of steps to a wide brick
walk leading to a small, wrought iron fountain and
lined with clipped boxwoods. Two paths led with
geometrical precision from the fountain, leading toward vistas she could not see. At the foot of the
trim shrubbery was an edging of violets, their
drooping purple blooms diffusing a delicate scent
on the air.

"The loggia catches the evening sun, madame,
and has protection from the wind. We spend much
time here at this season of the year." It was Anatole who answered once again, his voice carrying a
tone as cultured as that of any town beau. He had
none of the Gumbo, the combination of French with
the African dialect and a bit of English and Indian
thrown in for good measure, that had become the
language of the slaves.

Catching her look of swift surprise, Justin said,
"Anatole was educated with me in France. He was
my boy, given to me on my tenth birthday. My father needs him more now, not so much for the service, though it is important, as for the
understanding, the loyalty money cannot buy. Isn't
that so, Anatole?"

"Yes, Monsieur Justin," the dark man replied,
his lids lowered over his narrow eyes, his close-
cropped head held erect on his squared shoulders.

Claire felt pity for the man who must allow his
servant to speak and act for him. How humiliating
it must be to be forced to sit mute. To be bathed
and dressed and fed, and moved around from place
to place like a large human doll.

Justin asked after his father's health and spoke
for a moment of the planting going on in the fields,

of the illnesses among the hands, the usual spring fevers and ague, and of a mysterious sickness that had overtaken a number of the mules. They seemed to have forgotten her presence, but Claire did not care. She was happy to be relieved of the necessity of making conversation.

Two men came into view, walking along the garden path, as she stared idly out over the back yard. One was dressed as a gentleman in a fine lawn shirt, gloves, and cravat, and carried his coat over his arm. He was not quite as tall as Justin but he bore a slight resemblance to him about the nose and chin. He was broad shouldered and just missed being stocky. He carried his hat in his hand, and the waves of his brown hair caught the sun. His hazel eyes were narrowed against the bright light as he glanced up, just before he began to mount the stairs.

The man who strode beside him was obviously not of his class. He wore his brown shirt open at the throat, exposing a tuft of sandy hair that matched that which straggled from beneath the hat clamped upon his head. His unshaven cheek bulged with a chew of tobacco, and his pale blue eyes were frankly appraising as he stared at Claire. An American of Irish descent, or possibly English, she thought, certainly not a Creole, a Frenchman or Spaniard born in the new world.

He stopped on the steps with one foot propped higher than the other and his fist resting on his knee, while the other man came toward her, a smile in his eyes.

"Claire, my cousin Edouard, and our overseer, Ben Gannon," Justin introduced them.

The overseer lifted his hat fractionally, then looked on with an expression of derision as Edouard bowed over her hand, allowing his lips to touch it lightly since she was a married woman.

"My pleasure, Claire. I am very sorry for your accident that has prevented our meeting before now. You are better?"

This was the kind of gallantry to which she was accustomed. Claire replied easily.

While she was speaking, the overseer looked past her to Justin. "There's a problem down in the swamp needs your attention, if you can spare the time, Mr. Leroux. I was just coming up to see you when I met up with Ed here."

"Of course. Forgive me, Claire," her husband said perfunctorily. "I won't be long."

Claire looked after him, and there was a short lull in the conversation as Edouard saw she was not attending. In the silence, one of the bells on the back wall above their heads began to jangle on its coiled spring. Unconsciously, perhaps because of the noise, the overseer's voice rose, coming to them plainly.

"—be happy to take that high yeller article off your hands. Mighty purty, she is."

Though he said not a word, the negative shake of Justin's head and the cold stare he gave the other man was equally plain.

It was a moment before Claire realized what the overseer was referring to, then she knew. Belle-Marie. And as she felt the ripple of consternation that made the three men near her seem to freeze with their eyes on her face, she knew they realized it also. A hot wave of color flooded her cheeks and she could feel the sting of tears, tears of humiliation, behind her eyes.

"Well," Edouard said heartily, "I could stand a cup of coffee and one or two of those cakes Cook makes. What about the rest of you?"

"I will see to it, Monsieur Edouard," Anatole murmured and glided away down the steps toward the kitchen building to the right of the garden.

"You—you are Berthe's son, I think?"

"Yes. You have met mother?"

"This morning. She is a widow, I think?" How stupid. She knew the answer to that and she had not intended to mention it, but the thing had come out, the first thought to enter her head to keep the conversation going.

"My father has been dead some ten years."

"And you are Justin's cousin. I must not forget," she said, trying for a lighter vein. "So many new family relationships to remember can be so confusing."

"You will be fine, I know. You are the kind of person who makes only the most charming mistakes," he answered.

"Thank you. I can see that, like Justin, you have your share of the Leroux address, though you are not so much like him to look at."

He gave a mock sigh. "I'm afraid I take after my mother's people, while Justin favors the black Lerouxs, something I have always held against him. Down through the years they have been devils but charming enough to get away with it. My father was another one."

"Oh?"

"You will have to ask mother to show you her

portrait of my father. You will enjoy the painting as a fine piece of art as well as getting some idea of the family face." He laughed. "Of course you have a good example of it in Justin, or would have, if it weren't for his scar."

To hear it mentioned so casually made Claire draw in her breath. Again, there was an infinitesimal movement of the head of the paralyzed man. Claire, looking at him, thought for a fleeting moment there was something like concern for her in those faded gray eyes, the color of his thinning hair. Her father-in-law had also a gray complexion that made him seem all of the same color, a monotone portrait, an impression emphasized by his stillness.

Claire murmured something, having little curiosity about the painting of the man Justin had killed. But it seemed incredible that Edouard could mention so casually his father and the man who had killed him in the same breath.

A maid servant came hurrying along the path from the quarters a short distance away to the left, hidden by the branches of the trees. She climbed the steps breathlessly, a plump young girl with a timid look. Bobbing a curtsey by way of a greeting to those gathered on the loggia, she went on into the house. Helene's maid, she thought as a part of her mind registered in memory the tone of the bell that had rung minutes before.

"You look puzzled," Edouard said.

"Do I?" she fenced, not wanting to bring up what must be a painful subject, but unable for a moment to find another with which to distract him. Then something occurred to her.

"I wonder if you could tell me—about Justin's

scar? I don't like to ask him. He—it is a sensitive subject."

He smiled ruefully, looking at her, then his hazel eyes turned serious. "I rather suspect that you have another matter in mind. From the expression on your face I thought you were wondering why Justin and I aren't at daggers drawn. The reason has to do with the scar he carries. You see, I gave it to him."

"Oh, I'm sorry," Claire said, a flush on her cheekbones. "If you would rather not speak of it—"

"It isn't to my credit, but I don't mind. It happened a long time ago, when we were boys. We were playing at war, Justin with his army of slaves' children, I with mine. We had wooden swords, cudgels of dead limbs, and rawhide shields. All very serious. Justin and I were close to the same age, I have a few months on him, but I was also big for my age. My parents were more lenient with me too, and I was allowed to have a pocket knife. A lot of planning went into those mock wars, and there was a good bit of feeling, rivalry, pride, and anger in them too or things would never have come to the pass they did. Justin had established a fort down in the swamp. My army overran his position, and he and one or two others were fighting to cover the retreat of his main force."

He glanced at Claire and she nodded to show she understood.

"Well, the upshot was that Justin was disarmed and captured. It had been a long, hard, hot battle and I—I was elated. It wasn't often that I won. I told Justin that I was going to brand him as my captive."

She made a small sound of distress and he shook his head. "I know it sounds cruel, but children are cruel—I don't think I really meant it. I wanted Justin to finally admit defeat. I should have known he wouldn't. He lay there on the ground with four of my soldiers holding him down, and he stared at me with that arrogant look in his eyes, damning me. For one moment I went blind with pure, animalistic blood-lust, that and a determination to best him. I hated him because—ah, for a number of reasons that seemed important at the time, but chief among them was the knowledge that he was a better soldier, a better general, if you will, and that he knew it and knew I did too. If he had moved, had made a sound, I might have spared him, but he did not. He just lay there looking at me. Then it was over. I saw the blood running into the ground and I was sick, really sick. And I've lived with regret ever since. So you see, I know only too well how a man can be pushed into an affair of honor and how closely regret follows. Not that I'm making myself out to be a model of forgiveness, for I'm not. But daggers-drawn is a tiring pose to hold for any length of time. We live and life goes on and the whole thing hardly seems worth the pain."

"*C*—for captive," she said, staring without seeing out over the back garden.

"You would think that, wouldn't you? And it did start out that way. But they were retreating, you see. What I dislike myself most for was the thing I told Justin that day, and have never spoken of since. The *C* was for coward."

The sound of his voice, husky with remorse, was all at once an irritant. She remembered the evening she and Justin had met and his rejection of her pity. His attitude was more understandable, as was his sensitivity on the subject. Remembering suddenly that Marcel was perfectly able to hear and understand despite his paralysis, she turned toward him, appalled at what he might be feeling to hear his son discussed with such intimacy. Then she sighed, relieved. His eyes were closed, and if he was not asleep, he gave no sign that he had heard.

"You mustn't worry," Edouard told her in a low voice. "He often falls into these sudden naps."

Within a few minutes, Anatole brought the coffee tray. For the sake of politeness, Claire started to sip the rich, dark brew, and taste of the cakes Edouard recommended. But soon the atmosphere in the loggia grew too heavy to bear, and with a show of confidence in the strength that she was far from feeling, she rose and excused herself.

Marcel, awake now, looked at her with wide eyes, and Anatole inquired softly, "Should madame not wait for Monsieur Justin?"

"No, no. I will manage well enough by myself. But I appreciate your concern." And smiling brightly, declining the offer of Edouard's arm, she moved into the house.

She was fine until she reached the salon. But there a wave of dizziness assailed her and she stopped and closed her eyes, holding to the back of a walnut settee covered with gold brocade.

"Don't you feel well, Claire?" a soft voice said at her elbow. "You must lie down at once. Octavia will be furious to find you up and on your own. Come, it's just a step or two to my room."

"No, really. I will just stand here a moment."

"I wouldn't dream of allowing it," Berthe insisted, putting a surprisingly strong arm about her waist and leading her away. "My room opens here, on the front of the house, beside the salon. So convenient. You may lie on my bed and I will bring my vinaigrette before I send someone for Justin. He must carry you back to your room. Why you thought you were well enough to be up is beyond me. There is no need for such hurry. It is not as if Octavia would allow you to help her manage the house. She is quite jealous of her position and I am persuaded she would not permit it. There you are. Isn't that better?"

It was not. She did not wish to be rescued from this room by her husband. She hated the thought of what he would say. She wanted to get to her room by herself, but her weakness filled her with dismay.

"You must relax," Berthe told her, taking a rocking chair beside the fireplace and picking up the square of quilting she was piecing together. "It will be a few minutes before the girl arrives. I think the only bells in this house that are answered quickly are those of Justin and Helene. And yours, of course. We are so happy to have you here, all of us, including the servants. We had almost decided that Justin would never marry. He had never shown any inclination to do so in the past. Now we may only hope that my Edouard follows his good example and brings home a lovely girl like you. This has too long been a house of adults."

Claire looked away from those avid eyes, hazel like her son's, and encountered a hard, black stare. It came from a portrait above the fire burning in the fireplace, the portrait that Edouard had mentioned. Justin. Justin without a scar. She knew it was not, but she could not prevent the thought from burning in her mind. It was an oil of a man in the heavily-frilled shirt, the ruby-colored coat and intricate lace cravat of the decade just before the turn of the century. The background was dark, emphasizing his piercing black eyes and the look of indifference combined with a cynical smile and an obvious hauteur that gave him also the look of a fallen angel, a prince of darkness. In his long, slim fingers he held a snuff box with its lid encrusted with seed pearls and rubies.

"My husband, Gerard," Berthe informed her in a soft voice, then she went on when Claire did not comment, "And this is the snuff box he is holding. He enjoyed snuff. It was never an elegant habit. Few indulge any more. I have every snuff box he owned, one to match each suit of clothes to the number of thirty-seven."

It was not hard to believe. A pair of tables near the fireplace held innumerable tiny boxes, some glittering silver and gold with elaborate chasing. There were enameled boxes, painted ones with miniatures or French landscapes, jeweled boxes, boxes with wooden inlay or covered with satin, and even one of black enamel picked out in gold in the shape of a tiny coffin. For use with mourning, Claire assumed, conquering a strange quiver of combined distaste and amusement.

Then as she let her gaze move over the room she saw that the snuff boxes were not the only relics of her late husband that his widow had kept. Near the foot of the bed was a collection of canes, ebony, malacca or ivory with silver and gold handles, standing in a large china vase, interspersed with a number of riding crops. Shirt studs were gathered like precious jewels on a piece of velvet in an open stud box. On an *étagère* in a corner his peruques, in long and short styles in his natural black color and also dress white still showing traces of powder, were displayed. His clothes, Claire was almost sure, still filled the armoire, with his boots carefully polished and sitting beneath them.

"You are surprised that I still cherish my husband's things?" Berthe asked. "I enjoy having them around me. It makes it seem as if he has just stepped out or has gone into town, perhaps, and will soon be back." Her voice trailed away into nothing. She put down her sewing and began to wander about the room.

"These are the studs he wore in his wedding suit, and this is the snuff box I bought him for our tenth wedding anniversary. He seldom used it but he kept it by him all those years. But you are not interested. Perhaps this now, I don't believe you noticed it." She lifted a bronze object from the table beside the bed. She was right. Claire had not really looked at it. She had thought in a vague way that it was a notions box or some such thing.

"What is it?" she asked faintly.

"Don't you recognize it? Most people do so at once, it is such a striking likeness." With a timid eagerness Berthe glanced from the picture of Gerard over the mantle to the object she held in her hand.

"I don't—"

"It is a death mask, of course. Did you never see one? The idea is not new. Why, during the revolution in France it was the thing to buy a death mask of the aristocrats dying on the guillotine. A woman sat at the foot of the scaffold and as the head rolled into the basket she would catch it and mold it then and there. I had the doctor who attended my husband mold his dear features for me in wax after his death, then, when I went next to New Orleans, I had the wax cast in bronze. It shows every line, every brow and lash, even the grain of his skin. I cannot tell you how much comfort I have derived from it."

And there it was, the exact face of a man who had been dead more than ten years; the molding of his nose, the sensuous smoothness of his lips with their cynical twist. Like Justin, and yet with an expression in death her husband's face had never worn.

An odd feeling of near panic swept over Claire. She swung her feet over the side of the bed and pulled herself erect by clinging to the post. It was with relief that she heard a knocking sound on the outside french window that corresponded to the one in her own room. Then Justin stepped inside.

"Anatole said I would find—" he began, then as he saw Claire standing and wavering slightly with perspiration beading her upper lip, he moved forward and swept her into his arms.

"I am so glad you came, Justin," she murmured as she felt the cool evening air against her face. And, for the moment, she meant it.

The days passed, merging into weeks. And in those days the thought of the *gris-gris* found beneath her bed was seldom far from her mind, for instead of getting better, from that day she seemed to grow steadily more weak. It was not often that she felt completely well. She had little appetite and though she forced herself to eat the tempting meals Rachel brought to increase her strength, the food did no good. She lost weight until her eyes appeared huge in her pale face and the least noise or unexpected movement made her jump, every nerve in her body tingling.

She was left more and more to her own company and that of the great black cat whose name, she had discovered, was Bast. "Because it gives me a great satisfaction to look at Berthe's face when I say it, and to see in her eyes what she thinks I am going to say," Octavia had explained. "And you needn't tell me that the deity of that name that the Egyptians worshipped was female. I know that, but Bast, poor boy, does not. And it seems so supremely appropriate but for that small cavil. He is a sorry thing, but one I can claim as my own." She had smiled fondly on the cat, but the timbre of her voice had been oddly defiant.

And so he slept on the foot of Claire's bed, draped over her feet like a living shawl. He shared the bones of her meal with her, and as often as not, padded along behind her when she was carried to the loggia.

Justin was gone for longer and longer periods of time, out under the strengthening sun. His olive skin, always dark, took on a swarthy cast, and the scar standing out pale against his tanned face gave him the villainous look of a pirate. Gradually he lost that look of dissipation around his mouth caused by too little sleep, late hours in smoke filled rooms, and too much to drink. But at night he stretched out on the single bed at the foot of her own with a sigh of exhaustion.

During the daylight hours it was easy to see that there was no alternative to their arrangement, no other room where he could have slept. But sometimes, when, after lying in bed all day, she could not sleep, she lay beneath the mosquito netting that enclosed both beds together in a gauze prison and her thoughts grew morbid. It seemed that, like some medieval chatelaine, she was being guarded. Justin lay at her feet between her and the door. Whether he guarded her against harm or against escape she could not decide.

Once during the night she had been awakened by a scream. She had sat up, her heart beating fast, uncertain if the sound had been real or a lingering remnant of a dream. At the rustle of her bedclothes Justin awoke.

"What is it?" he asked, his voice vibrant with a quiet strength in the dark.

"I—I thought I heard someone cry out," she explained, beginning to feel foolish.

They listened together, then just as she opened her mouth to apologize for waking him for nothing the keening scream came again.

Justin chuckled softly. "It's only a panther down in the swamp, *chère*. Go back to sleep."

She heard him turn over in his narrow bed, then she lay back on her own pillows, thinking of the gentle endearment he had used and smiled ironically as she remembered her pity, so long ago, for the girls who married men who carried them off to homes in the wilds where alligators roared and panthers shattered the night with their cries. Abruptly she shivered, and, pulling the sheet up to her chin, lay staring wide-eyed into the dark.

They had been married the week before Fat Tuesday. Lent came and went, as did Holy Week and Easter. Then summer was upon them, in fact, if not by the calendar.

"My dear Claire, I don't care for the way you are looking," Octavia said one morning. "I have always considered that too much bed rest is not good. For myself, it saps my strength. A month, now, would be enough to put me near the grave! I haven't liked to suggest that you get up, Justin has been so set against it. But you are weaker than I like, even if it is the fashion, though I must admit you are in looks. Your eyes are bright, and your skin is positively translucent. But I would feel much better if you had a trifle more color. What do you say to a short carriage drive?"

"Oh, I would like that above anything."

"It is sure to improve your appetite. You needn't pretend to me. I saw you give your gumbo dinner to Bast. He loves shrimp, of course, but you really must not. He will get fat, and I cannot bear an obese cat."

"I—all at once I could not eat another mouthful, though it was deliciously seasoned, and I didn't like to hurt Cook's feelings."

"Very commendable, I'm sure, but you need it, and Bast is an excellent mouser and it will make him lazy, though he looks thin enough now, doesn't he? Come, put on one of your fresh muslins and I will send to the stables to have the carriage brought round."

By the time Claire was dressed, the carriage was waiting at the front steps; a landau with a new coachman on the box replacing the man who had been killed. Helene and Berthe, hearing of the expedition, had decided to join them, and the four ladies stepped into the carriage. They set out down the drive, a mere track paved with shells and overhung with moss-draped trees.

"Where are we going?" Claire wanted to know, staring back at the house that looked so cool and comfortable at the top of the slope that led up from the bayou curving around it.

"Just a short drive about the plantation. We won't be leaving our own roads. I thought you might enjoy seeing the fields, the quarters where our people live, their church, that sort of thing," Octavia replied.

Claire nodded, agreeing that she would be interested in seeing the outbuildings and the land.

"Are you quite all right, dear?" Berthe asked diffidently. "The motion of the carriage does not bother you? I don't wish to sound inquisitive, but my maid tells me that your Rachel has let it be known that you are not eating well and sometimes suffer from *des nausées*—the illness of the morning."

"Not *enceinte* already!" Helene exclaimed. "You need not have hurried so. I have no wish to dandle my grandchildren on my knee."

"But—I couldn't be!" Claire said, finding her voice at last.

"Oh, there has been time enough," Helene assured her, shrugging pettishly. "Personally, I would have thought—but there, that is Justin. No consideration for anyone other than himself. Marcel never considered my feelings."

"Helene!"

"I do wish you wouldn't say that, Berthe, really I do," her sister-in-law told her without removing her gaze from the carriage window.

"Well, my Gerard was always the soul of—"

"Nor prattle of Gerard, always your Gerard, either," she requested in a strained voice.

Claire paid little attention to their wrangling. What could she say? How could she tell them why it was impossible for her to be pregnant? She could not. And so she remained silent. Let them think what they pleased, she thought, they would find out soon enough.

Sensing, perhaps, a portion of her embarrassment, Octavia intervened with a change of subject, and the other ladies talked of various things, their voices raised slightly above the sound of the wheels.

They rode through a short stretch of forest, then open country began; meadows green with oats where cattle and horses grazed, fields of young corn trembling in the breeze and then rows of sugar cane, mile upon mile, of different heights, some new, just pushing above the black earth, some knee high, and some higher already than a man's head. The sun beat down, building up the heat inside the carriage, and dust filtered in, a fine grit, settling in the folds of their dresses and on the fine film of perspiration that appeared on their faces.

The road they were traveling appeared to make a wide circle around the perimeter of the plantation. As they began the last loop back toward Sans Songe, the country once again grew thickly wooded and they were grateful for the coolness. Several times they crossed small rumbling bridges over the tributaries of the bayou. Trees towered above them that had never felt the bite of an ax, and grape-vines as thick as a man's wrist reached toward the sun at their tops. Saw briars pushed also toward the light that glimmered high above, light that was denied entrance to the forest floor by the close-knitted tree tops. But beneath that leafy canopy, the ground covered with a thick, sound-deadening coverlet of leaves was fairly clear, the small under-growth shaded out by the intertwined branches above. Here the road was a mere track, wide enough for only one vehicle, with grass and weeds and small saplings trying to grow in the middle be-tween the ruts, sweeping the underside of the carriage as they passed over them.

A thick silence closed around them. In the suffo-cating stillness, they became aware of the miasma of the swamp, the smell of dankness and stagnant mud.

Suddenly, the carriage was invaded by a swarm of mosquitoes and they slapped at them, crushing them, fanning them out the windows of the fast rolling coach.

"Why in heaven's name did anyone ever build a road through here?" Claire asked, slapping at a mosquito that had been totally unimpressed by their attempts to evict him.

"It was cut originally so that the laborers could bring the cypress wood for the big house from the swamp. Every board, every joist, was grown right here on our own land and cut, stacked, seasoned, shaped and pegged into place by our own people."

"Really?" Claire asked with interest, staring at the trees that soared skyward, trees that were, or so it seemed, as old as time, crowded about with the curiously human-looking natural stumps known as cypress knees. Once again the bayou came into view, a deep but narrow stream here, a cut into the flat earth of the forest floor.

"How did they get such huge trees out of the swamp?"

"With oxen teams, often as many as eight in a span. The lumber for the houses in the quarters, the outbuildings, the hospital, jail, copperage, stables, barns, nursery, the church for our people, for everything, right down to the corncribs, was grown here on our land. It gives one a great sense of accomplishment only to look at it all. You will see it on the final part of our drive. We will return through the quarters."

They rattled on a few minutes more and then Berthe spoke. "Is this where they think the panther roams?"

"So I would imagine." It was Helene who answered her.

"So close to the house?"

Helene frowned at her as if wondering what in the world had made her bring up such a subject.

"It stands to reason that it must be if we can hear him from the house in the night," Octavia said shortly.

Claire found herself searching the shadows for the beast, a feeling of fascinated dread gripping her, then she was jerked out of that pastime as the carriage ground to a halt.

"What in the name of Satan?" Helene exclaimed,

clutching at the window frame to save herself from
an ignominious fall. Berthe squealed and caught
Octavia's arm, then as the other woman shook her
off impatiently so that she could thrust her head
out the window, she subsided into a corner of the
coach with an injured expression on her pale face.

"Oh," Octavia said, going very still.

"Well?" Helene demanded.

Still Octavia did not speak. There was a sudden
flurry of shouts and curses from the driver, the
coach bucked, lurching to the side of the narrow
road, then the wheels of their carriage scraped those
of another. A pair of cream horses pulling a yellow
curricle crowded by them.

On the seat was one of the most flamboyant figures Claire had ever seen. She knew instantly who
it was. Belle-Marie, Justin's quadroon mistress. After that one encompassing glance she turned her
head, staring hard in front of her, thinking that the
woman would pass them by. But the curricle pulled
up when its driver was even with the windows of
the carriage.

She was the color known as *café au lait*, coffee
with milk, a warm cream brown with a luminous
quality to her skin. Her cheekbones were high, with
a hint of Indian blood, and across them was a flush
of color like the blush on a ripe peach. Her brows
were winged arches of dark silk and beneath them
were sloe-shaped pools of brown. Black hair was
pulled back and covered by an orange silk turban
boasting a gilt brooch of intricate, far-eastern design, a holder for a white ostrich plume that arched
gracefully to fall to eye level, floating as she moved
her head. In her ears dangled gold hoops, and her

dress of soft peach muslin left her shoulders bare. She was so beautiful, even with her tawdry jewels and barbaric colors, that Claire felt her throat tighten with some difficult emotion that had nothing to do with admiration.

An insolent smile on her lush mouth, Belle-Marie inclined her head. "I hope I see you well."

"Yes, of course," Claire answered, though she was by no means sure that she should dignify this meeting with a reply. Would Justin be angry that she had stopped to bandy words with his mistress? Would it make any difference that it was Belle-Marie who had forced them to stop? Would he be inclined to side with his wife or his mistress in this situation? Claire thought she knew he would support her only if she acted as society expected.

"And how do you fare at Sans Songe, a city girl from *belle* Nouvelle Orléans?"

"As well, I'm sure, as you." Claire was unable to bear that knowing smile.

"Oh, but I am not of New Orleans. You could not know, of course, but I was born on Sans Songe."

"Indeed?"

"Certainement. My parents were freed some years ago."

Claire saw the implication, that Justin had given her parents' freedom to Belle-Marie as a gift.

When she was sure that Claire was not going to comment, the quadroon continued. "I am one with Sans Songe; the swamp was my playground until the age of fifteen. I never worked, for here the children do not labor, though, of course, when I grew older I was given a—position—"

Still Claire did not answer. She could not find a word to say in the face of such effrontery.

"Why does the coachman not drive on?" Helene demanded, suddenly finding her voice. There was an echo of the question in Claire's own mind.

"You must not blame the man," Belle-Marie informed them with a careless laugh, "I fear our wheels are locked."

"Insolent chit! Back your curricle at once so that we may proceed!"

"Oh, I shall, in good time. First there is a thing that is in my heart to say to Madame Leroux—the younger. You see, madame, I have this great fear, me, that Sans Songe is an unhealthy place for you."

"Why you!" Octavia exclaimed with the ferocity of one who had held her tongue as long as humanly possible.

"Claire, you are within your rights to have this—this vulgar person whipped, and so I would, if I were you. She grows entirely too sure of herself."

"By all means," Belle-Marie flashed, "though I think it would be wise to ask Monsieur Justin first."

Claire heard Berthe gasp yet again. Helene sat forward. "I will have it done then. I am not afraid of my son's anger!"

"Perhaps not, madame, but I have knowledge of another thing, a family—affair."

Helene made a low sound in her throat, but Belle-Marie did not wait to see how the older woman would react to her jeer. She turned back to Claire.

"Sans Songe is not a safe place, madame, as I think you have discovered. It is possible that it will become even less safe if you should stay."

"I quite understand your feelings," Claire said,

meeting those dark, liquid eyes with her own level gaze, "but I was brought up to believe that a woman's place was at her husband's side, that a man and wife are two parts of a whole. And so I would not dream of leaving Sans Songe—or my husband!"

Chapter Six

CLAIRE LAY BACK in the tub of warm, scented water and thought of the meeting on the road that afternoon. She could not dismiss it from her mind. What had made her declare herself unable to leave Justin's side? Was it simply pique, anger at the unbelievable insolence of Belle-Marie and a contrary determination not to be influenced by her barbaric attempts to frighten her? Or was there something deeper involved, something other than duty? It was not a question she cared to face.

Fretfully, she squeezed the sponge of loofah-fiber dry and began to scrub with it. The sound of a door closing came to her, and she twisted her head toward the sound beyond the tall, wooden screen covered with painted muslin that surrounded her, closing in the warmth from the small fire in the fireplace and protecting her from drafts.

"Rachel?" she called. She had dismissed the girl, weary of her constant attendance.

"No." The voice was deep and rough. Justin, and not in the best of moods from the sound. She opened her mouth to ask him to leave the room, then shut it.

"You are back early," she said instead.

"Too early, it seems." There was no humor in his voice.

"I—I won't be long. We went for a drive this afternoon and the roads were so dusty—"

"I have been hearing about this drive."

A wave of depression swept over Claire. He was angry, and, as she had expected, at her. Still she managed to suffuse her voice with a careless coolness as she answered.

"Oh?"

"Yes. Tell me, how does it come about that you are *enceinte?*"

How she wished that she could laugh gaily and pass it off as an amusing tale, but no, she could not. Hot color burned her face. There was a constriction in her throat and she barely managed to speak at all.

"I'm not," she murmured, staring at the soap-clouded water of her bath.

"No? It is odd then that Berthe has the distinct impression that you are."

"It was Rachel. She told your aunt's maid that I was often ill of a morning. You know how servants gossip. And I simply could not explain that—that it could not be."

Embarrassment made it impossible for her to sit still a moment longer, and she felt so vulnerable in her undressed state. Rising abruptly, she swung a towel hanging on the rim of the tub about her and stepped out. "Would you please hand me my dressing gown," she requested. "It is on the foot of the—"

She halted as Justin, one hand on the standing screen, wordlessly held out her wrapper. She took it, then shut her mouth in a thin line, while with the other hand she clutched the towel about her. They stared at each other in mutual suspicion and distrust.

"So," he said at last, "you have been ill in the morning. You have managed to hide it from me."

"Only because you leave so early for the fields. In any case, it was only a feeling of nausea, not so great a thing."

"For how long?"

"Since—since that revolting voodoo symbol was placed under my bed. I have tried—truly I have—to tell myself it is all silly superstition, but this sickness persists."

"Are you quite sure? If I remember you did not protest so very much for someone marrying a stranger. I fully expected it to be necessary for you to be put on bread and water and locked in your room for a month before you consented. It would not be the first time a man had been duped. Are you certain there was nothing more than cousinly affection between you and the man you were all set to marry, what was his name? Jean-Claude?"

The flush of anger slowly died out of her face leaving it as pale as carved ivory.

"I would give you my word, but I doubt that you would believe me."

"Clever of you," he said in a voice devoid of emotion.

"Perhaps you would prefer to—" she began with angry dignity.

"Yes, I think I would," he agreed, and moving with deceptive grace, he pulled her into his arms.

She did not resist. At the back of her mind she knew it would be fatal to try. His kiss was neither gentle nor cruel, and though it had a quality of exploration, it seemed more designed to impress upon her his calm and deliberate passion.

She wanted to remain as cool and unmoved as a vestal virgin, but she found the strength leaving her, so that she yielded, swaying against him, her lips molded to his. She scarcely heard the faint tap on the door and then the voice of Rachel asking if she was required to help her mistress to dress.

Justin thrust her from him, and as Rachel appeared around the side of the screen, it was a moment before Claire could attend to her, so lost was she in receding emotions. Then a secret amusement sprang into her eyes. The wetness of her arms had imprinted themselves on the front of Justin's shirt.

"Later," he promised her with a hard glance before he turned and strode from the room, slamming the door behind him.

Dropping the towel and moving slowly to slip her arms into the sleeves of her dressing gown, Claire noticed Rachel's too-stolid expression. How much had the girl gathered from what she had seen, she wondered, sighing, aware of the slight ache in her chest from the strength of Justin's arms. How much would Rachel tell of it, and to whom?

The maid brushed the dust of the road from her hair and braided it in a cool coronet. Then she passed the underdress of rose muslin over Claire's head and tied the tapes at the back. The overdress of transparent pink gauze came next, and with it Claire decided on impulse to wear, on a black velvet ribbon, the cameo Justin had given her in her wedding basket.

As she was being dressed Claire felt the nervousness in Rachel's manner, and the girl's attitude kept the scene with Justin before her mind. What was it she had said so impulsively; that her feeling of nausea had begun after the appearance of the *gris-gris*? Slowly a suspicion grew, a suspicion based on whispered stories heard over the years in the town where she had lived. In the old days, with the intrigues of the French court, poison had always been a possibility, the first thought at the onset of an unexplained illness. The habit of considering it had come naturally to New Orleans with the first French immigrants. Poison and intrigue had found a receptive climate in that warm city where labor was left to the slaves, leaving ample time for the quarrels and devious affairs that led to revenge in its quietest, surest form. Claire shivered a little, and touched the cameo at her throat, that of Louis XVII, the child king who was said to have been poisoned. Who would want to poison her? Would anyone have a reason? There was the quadroon, but surely she would not dare to go so far. No, she was frightening herself unnecessarily. She must be. But the thought would not leave her, and she was aware of a deep agitation when, a short while later, she walked out onto the back loggia.

She thought for a moment Justin was sitting with his father, then she sighed in unconscious relief as she recognized Edouard with his back to her.

He rose at once when he saw her, and offered her the chair in which he had been sitting beside her father-in-law.

She thanked him and, as she sat down and settled back, greeted Marcel as if she had no idea he could not answer. She thought she saw his eyelids flicker and a warmth come into his dark eyes at the sight of her. He was such undemanding company that she had grown fond of sitting with him, talking or not talking, as she pleased, in the past weeks. As she straightened her skirts, she smiled and nodded to Anatole, his patient shadow.

She could feel her nerves relax. With Marcel and Edouard, at least, she knew there would be no awkward questions about her supposed pregnancy. Marcel could not ask them, and convention forbade Edouard to speak of it. Even if she had been as large as a cow he could have done no more than ask after her health. It was strange to think of Justin speaking so frankly. He was her husband, of course, and in addition, not so bound by the code of the gentlemen. Or was that strictly true? He had treated her with altogether more consideration than she had expected, until this afternoon. But she must not think of it or she would be blushing and Edouard would not be human if he did not wonder why.

Edouard was not a very communicative person. Not since the first day she had met him had she really talked to him. She wondered if he regretted his confiding in her, or if he supposed that she held some grudge against him for being the cause of Justin's childhood scarring. She hoped her manner had not given him any such idea.

He was, it seemed, not much involved with the running of Sans Songe itself. He kept an eye on things while Justin was away, but his special interest was several hundred arpents of land given over to the cultivation of Sea Island cotton, a departure from the sugarcane that was the staple crop of the plantation. He was friendly enough, but rather self-effacing, spending the long evening hours in his room on the front side of the house. There did not seem to be much affection between himself and anyone else in the family, not even Berthe, his mother. They treated each other with a kind of distant civility, though at times Claire had seen Berthe stare after him, a curious expression of sadness on her face. But then Berthe enjoyed the role of tragedienne, Claire reminded herself; she liked to dramatize her life. And it seemed natural to suppose that she was only doing so when she looked at her fatherless son. Also, Edouard seemed to be a man with some strength of character and it was difficult to see why he chose to remain at Sans Songe, in a subordinate position. Why didn't he break away on his own, start his own plantation? Or failing that, at least live his own life, be his own man.

And then, so strong was this new habit of suspicion that it occurred to her to wonder if it was as simple as that. Perhaps Edouard had never left the house because it had not been to his advantage to do so. In the past, before Justin's marriage, it must have seemed that he, Edouard, would have a good chance of owning Sans Songe. What was the life expectancy of a rake hell, a man known to be hot of temper and quick to challenge? Who was there to benefit if he died? Marcel, it was true, was the owner, but what control could a paralyzed man past middle age exercise? And when Marcel was dead and Justin also, Edouard would inherit with Helene. And if even then the estate did not stay intact, half of the acreage belonging to the plantation was still a fortune making it worthwhile to play the hanger-on.

But was it worth killing for? The question echoed in her mind without volition. Worth ridding Justin of his new wife, a wife who might become a stabilizing influence, a wife who might provide an heir and remove Edouard from the succession?

Don't be unnecessarily stupid, she told herself angrily, and to make up for her lapse, she at once began to chatter with a forced brightness.

The sun was long down, the twilight hour, *l'heure bleue* of a southern spring was around them. The hour was advancing toward supper and she could smell the aromas that drifted from the small kitchen building, mingling with the lemon sweetness of honeysuckle growing beyond the confines of the garden. A few mosquitoes whined about them, enough to be annoying, but not yet the swarm that would come with full dark. She could see Edouard's face and his grave eyes as he talked.

"When my parents and Marcel first came here more than thirty years ago, this place really was a wilderness. The entire area that we are using now as fields was covered with virgin forest. Forest that had to be cleared slowly and at the cost of sweat and lives. There were no neighbors for a hundred miles or more, nothing but swamp, alligators, panthers, and savages. My mother was the only white woman between here and New Orleans for a while. Then more families, escaping the terror in France, accepted grants and moved out into the forest to become *sauvages nobles*. And then Marcel went to New Orleans and returned with a bride, Helene."

"A woman has to love her husband a great deal to brave the dangers of the wilderness."

"Yes, I suppose—" Edouard began, then broke off to exclaim, "Uncle Marcel, what is it?"

An alarming color had suffused his ordinarily pale face, and an expression of desperation filled his eyes as he tried to force sound, coherent sound, from his open mouth. But all that issued was an ineffectual croak that was so obviously an embarrassment to Marcel that Claire felt his shame and his rage as if it were her own. What was he trying to say? She had no idea, and from the look of sad concern on Anatole's face, neither did he. But as Marcel's struggle to voice his thoughts went on and on, she could bear it no longer.

"What is it, Anatole? What does he want?"

The dark servant shook his head. "I do not know madame. For so long a time, after the night he became like this, he would try to speak. No one could understand, not even I. And so he stopped. Now he begins again. It could be that he thinks you, maybe, will understand. You are *sympathique* and, I think, he likes you."

"I wish I could understand," she said, staring into Marcel's eyes, the pain of compassion in her voice. "I only wish I could."

For one more long moment her father-in-law held her eyes, then abruptly he ceased straining and relaxed against the cushions of his chaise, exhaustion graying his face.

After a moment of silence, Anatole spoke. "I will take him in now. He will wish to rest."

With Marcel gone, a feeling of strain came between Claire and Edouard, and as soon as she could without seeming too obvious, Claire excused herself and returned to the house.

Darkness had fallen, but it was still nearly an hour to the last meal of the day. Town hours were kept on the plantation, not so much to be fashionable as to take advantage of the cool of the evening. The salon was deserted and the settees, in the light of the girondoles burning on the mantel, had a forlorn look. The Leroux family was not a particularly close one, and the room was seldom used.

Claire was about to pass on through the room to the outside, then around the gallery to her own room, when she heard a sound. It was a woman, a woman crying. She stopped, undecided. It came, she was certain, from Berthe's room, and though she was reluctant to intrude, she was also reluctant to pass on without concern. She stepped to the door and turned the knob quietly, ready to offer her aid if Berthe had need of it, or to withdraw at once if there did not appear to be anything she could do.

The room was dark, the only light a pale glimmer from the candles behind Claire. At first she could see nothing, then, as her eyes gradually became accustomed to the dimness, she could make out the figure of a woman. She was standing in the center of the floor, her head bowed over an object she held in her hands, while her shoulders shook with her weeping. It was a soft, almost melodious grief, without hope of comfort.

Suddenly, the weeping woman became aware of the light, for she swung around. And Claire drew in her breath as she saw that it was not Berthe. It was Helene, a distraught Helene, clasping the death mask of Berthe's husband Gerard to her breast.

"Gloat!" she screamed. "Mealy-mouthed prig! You were never woman enough for him, never! You never knew him, not as I did. And for all your outward show, you can never mourn him as I do, or feel his loss—here in your heart—after all these years. And you're glad. You're glad, I know it! All this—" she flung out her arm to encompass the trophy-filled room. "All this is to mortify me. Deny it how you will. Except this—this travesty of his poor face. Why did you do this to him? Why, except to hurt me?" She pushed the death mask toward Claire.

What faint light there was coming from behind Claire left her face in shadow. It was little wonder, she supposed, that Helene, her eyes filled with tears, should mistake her for Berthe. But what to do about it? Go quietly away, or explain and let her suffer the chagrin of knowing a stranger had witnessed her outburst?

Without a word, Claire swung around, pulled the door to behind her, and fled.

As she went along the gallery nearing her room, she saw a light burning within. Justin would be inside, then. Her hands were still trembling, and her face, she knew must be pale with the shock of her discovery. Her footsteps slowed and she turned toward the railing, leaning against it while she tried to calm herself to present a cool, unmoved front to her husband.

Helene, that arrogant, time-ravaged beauty, had been in love with her husband's brother, so in love that ten years later she could still weep her heart out over a mask of his dead face. Her husband's brother, a married man with a son, a man who was shot to death in a duel with his nephew, Helene's own son!

Did everyone in the house know these terrible facts? If so, it was no wonder they were not particularly close.

As she stood there, she became aware of a distant rumble, like thunder, but much more regular. As it continued, she thought to herself that it sounded like the mutter of drums, such as she had heard often at night coming from Congo Square in New Orleans, where the slaves were permitted to dance to their African rhythms. The incessant beating, in both ceremony and thoughtless pleasure, had often lulled her to sleep.

"Listening to the drums? My girl tells me there is going to be a meeting down along the bayou back in the swamp."

Octavia stepped out of her darkened room and strolled to join Claire.

"A meeting?" Claire asked, suppressing a start at her sudden appearance.

"Voodoo. It's their religion, you know, brought with them from Africa. They worship the snake god, the Zombi or Vodu, as he is named. He gives them special powers, or so they believe. One of their legends, from the Dahomeyan tribe, I think, says that man and woman came into the world blind, and that it was the serpent, the Zombi, who gave them sight. Curious, isn't it? A direct contradiction of our belief that the serpent took away our paradise instead of giving it to us. Unless, of course, you consider that man was better off blind."

"How do you know all that?"

"I asked," Octavia stated forthrightly. "They don't like to talk about it. They have been told repeatedly that their beliefs are wicked and that ours is the only religion. But I am a persistent woman, and eventually they came to the conclusion that I am harmless." There was irony in her voice.

"You—you know of their *gris-gris?*"

"Certainly. They think they can make things happen by wishing evil or good. And as difficult as it may be to believe, it seems they can. The *gris-gris* they use does little more than symbolize the wish. A real Voodoo—or Voodooienne, the leader, priest or priestess, or what-have-you—doesn't really need a *gris-gris.* He can merely let it be known that he is contemplating the death of an individual for this or that reason, and the deed is done. The doomed one takes to his bed, and, in a matter of days, is dead. Often it isn't necessary for a believer of voodoo to know that he is being 'fixed.' Any illness is looked upon with deep suspicion, and if he can think of anyone who might have taken him into dislike, he goes immediately to the Voodoo for a darker magic." She shrugged. "It becomes an endless cycle."

"Then why do they use the *gris-gris?*"

"As I said, they are symbols, not unlike the cross, the holy water, the bones of the saints, bits of wood and river water, things not intrinsically sacred, but made so by our beliefs. So it is with theirs."

Claire blinked at such casual heresy. Then as the meaning sank in she said, "Yes." She could not keep a thoughtful tone from her voice. It was peculiar, finding that someone at Sans Songe knew of voodoo, when she herself had been a victim of the practice. Then she shook her head. What was she thinking of this evening? Why was her mind running on these lines? She knew who was behind the things that had happened to her. It was Belle-Marie. It must be.

"Ah well. I'm not sure I understand, myself. I think sometimes that true understanding of these things comes in the blood, or in the mother's milk. Don't upset yourself—what was that?"

It was a low noise, a gurgling growl in the throat. They stood listening as it went on and on, coming from Claire's room. Chill bumps rose on Claire's arms, and she swallowed hard before turning her eyes toward the older woman.

"I can't imagine," she began, but as the timbre rose to an animalistic shriek, Octavia interrupted her.

"Bast!" the older woman cried, hurrying forward to pull open the french windows. Hard on her heels, Claire searched the room with her eyes. There was no sign of Justin as she had expected. There was no one but the great black cat, squirming on the floor with a gelatinous froth dribbling from his mouth.

"Stay back," Octavia warned. "He doesn't know what he is doing. He might savage you."

"What is the matter with him?"

"Convulsions. It could be several things; disease, something he has eaten—"

Suddenly the cat stretched out on his side, shuddering violently. The sound in his throat had died to a whine, his eyes were tightly closed, but his lips were pulled back from his teeth in a grimace of pain.

"He—ate my dinner."

"Your dinner?"

"I was not hungry, and he begged so—"

Abruptly the cat went still and his eyes closed to slits. Octavia put her hand on his side, her fingers sinking into the black velvet of his fur.

"He is still breathing, I think. What is this?"

Her questing fingers had slipped beneath a loop of dirty brown string tied around his neck. As she tugged on it, a tiny bag came into view. Tipping its contents into her hand Octavia murmured, "Sand, a few slivers of bone, a pebble or two, pepper, it appears to be."

A terrible certainty came over Claire, though she could not have said from where it came or why it should seem so menacing.

"It's voodoo, isn't it?"

"Yes," Octavia whispered. "Voodoo."

Chapter Seven

"WILL YOU COME with me?"

The question, put so abruptly, caught Claire by surprise. "Come with you?"

"To the ceremony in the swamp. If the Voodooienne put the spell on Bast, she can take it off. She 'crossed' him, she can 'uncross' him, as they say. And she will, I'm sure, for a price."

"But—but couldn't you send for her?" Claire asked. The thought of the meeting, so primitive, and far beyond her experience, deep in the swamp, was not by any means attractive to her. She could not imagine herself setting out to find it among the moss-draped trees, along the damp trails.

"It may be too late. I must hurry," Octavia said, removing her shawl and carefully wrapping it around her pet before picking him up in her arms.

"Wait! Let's ask Justin."

"No! He would never give us his escort, not for something like this. And he would try to keep me from going. He thinks it all nonsense, and he thinks me a foolish old woman for crediting them with any kind of power. He would let Bast die! For the love of God, Claire. Don't stand there. Come on."

Claire did not like the edge of tightly controlled hysteria that she caught in the older woman's voice. "Octavia, are you certain?"

"Don't come then. I will go alone."

With her face hard, she pushed past Claire toward the door. Claire stared after her. She could not let her go alone, not into the black dangers of the swamp. She did not want to go, but her conscience would not allow her to stay.

"Just a minute," she called, and snatching up a spencer to cover her arms against the mosquitoes, she hurried after Octavia.

The house and the clear stretch of lawn around it were soon left behind. For a few yards they followed the road curving around the plantation, but when the house was no longer visible behind them, they plunged into the woods, following a small animal trail through the high weeds. Octavia seemed to know where she was going, for she took the lead with a fine unconcern for the possibility of snakes lurking on the path. Briars clawed at their skirts and ankles, and the branches of saplings whipped at their shoulders. Claire developed a stitch in her side, and her breathing grew ragged as her ribs began to throb with a dull ache.

They came to the deep woods where the virgin oaks and gums and ashes over their heads closed out the starlight. In that echoing space the sound of the drums was louder, and mingling with it they could hear sharp cries and the rising crescendo of voices chanting.

By now Octavia was almost running. Claire followed, paying more attention now to where she was putting her feet than to what lay ahead of them. A feeling of deep fatalism gripped her. Committed now to this escapade, there was no use looking back. She pushed her apprehension from her mind, stopped probing the darkness around them, and concentrated on keeping up with Octavia.

The black crevasse of the bayou appeared to their left and they moved along beside its banks in the easier going of the animal trail. Then suddenly there was a glow ahead of them through the trees. The throbbing of the drums seemed to be all around them, mixed with a cacophony of jingling, clashing, and rattling sounds. Then they saw the figures, entranced by the hypnotic beat, the night crowding in upon them, and the leaping flames of the giant fire, as they swayed in a dance from out of the steaming jungles of Africa, a dance out of time.

Octavia and Claire slowed and came to a halt at the edge of the clearing. Beyond the dancers, the fire was reflected in the looping curve of the bayou, and the light it threw skyward illuminated the green of the trees that encircled the open space and washed the stars from the patch of heaven above them. The ground was smooth, beaten flat and hard by the pounding of countless feet.

"If you will stay here," Octavia whispered, "I will see if I can get a word with the priestess. She will be more likely to do as I ask if you aren't with me.

She doesn't know you to trust you, and I expect she would be suspicious. I don't want you to be too mixed up in this. Justin will be angry enough if he discovers that I persuaded you to bear me company."

It seemed reasonable. Claire nodded.

"Stay back out of sight here, among the trees. I don't suppose these people, most of whom are our own workers and know you by sight, would dream of harming you under normal circumstances, but they are not normal now. They are drunk with the night and the drums in their blood, besides a generous supply of homemade liquor unless I miss my guess. It is forbidden, of course, but nonetheless evident for all that. At these times passion—runs high. Take care."

"Don't worry. I won't show my face."

"Good."

With that single word, the older woman turned and drifted away through the trees just outside the perimeter of the circle. Claire drew back further into the shadows. Then from behind the screen of branches she watched, her heartbeat slowly rising with disbelief.

Most of the people in the clearing were dressed in their work clothes, the women in shapeless dresses and the men in breeches of rough cloth, but with their feet bare. But several of them, those nearest the fire, wore loin cloths of red material, and on their wrists, knees, and ankles, leather thongs strung with bells, beads, and animal teeth. Several shook gourd rattles, and small bags, like the one found on Bast, bounced on their chests. Their skins glistened like ebony with sweat and oil, and the orange light of the fire ran in highlights over them. To one side, three men hunkered over barrels with leather stretched over the top, pounding them with the flat of their hands in a constant rhythm, while a fourth used a pair of thick wooden sticks to hammer a hollowed-out log. Near the fire was a box with holes drilled in the sides for air, a small wire cage holding several half-grown roosters, and a great iron cauldron from which rose clouds of steam.

How long she watched she did not know. Time seemed less than nothing. But then, from the shadows near the bayou, a woman appeared. At once the drums stopped, the people grew still and backed away to the edges of the clearing, leaving her alone in the center.

She was of middle age, a large woman with well-rounded arms and face, clad in a long dress of tent-like proportions in a pure white that seemed to glow. She held up her arms, and a single drum began a slow, measured cadence. She began to move from side to side with a grace surprising in one of her bulk, and with each step the bells on her ankle bracelets made a musical chatter.

A tall, gangling man in a loin cloth ran from one side. He lifted the lid of the box Claire had noticed earlier, and from its depths drew forth a great snake, larger and longer than any she had ever seen. It was as big around as the man's arm and twice as long as he was tall.

"Le Grande Zombi!" the man cried out as the serpent coiled himself slowly about his uplifted arm

and opened round, black eyes, gazing unwinkingly around him.

"*Le Zombie—*" the crowd breathed.

Claire's scalp prickled and she swallowed, as the big woman, obviously the high priestess, the Voodooienne, accepted the snake and allowed it to coil along her arm and about her neck and upper body. Crooning as to a baby, she turned and swayed, moving around the circle, gently undulating her massive hips, a rapt look on her face. Gradually the tempo increased, her movements became more vigorous and her eyes grew large with a growing excitement.

Tension built in the crowd. They inched toward the Voodooienne, slowly closing in on her. The woman's mouth fell open, her eyes became unfocused. Her lips moved, forming a single word, little more than a whisper.

"Power."

"Power, power, power—she got the power, power, power—" It ran around the circle, a whisper rising to a chant.

Now the woman was jerking, her body shaken by spasms that ran like ripples over her. The great green-black body of the snake seemed larger, more prominent against the white of her dress, and he seemed to be awakening as the frenzy grew in the woman holding him.

Then suddenly, another woman broke through the crowd to the inner circle. A young woman. A woman whose cream-colored skin caught the fireglow, caught it on her arms, her legs, and her shoulders, for she wore nothing more than a single strip of red cloth twisted about her breasts and hips with the free end caught by a small dagger thrust through the material. A rag on the same cloth held her hair, that was loose upon her shoulders, back from her face. And she threw back her head to let it swing as wild and free as the dusky goddess it crowned.

With a cruel smile twisting her lips, she placed both hands on the older priestess' arms and pushed her backward. With a full throated cry she leaped high, then she began to dance.

"Belle-Marie, she got the power. She stole the power—power—power—"

And it appeared that she had seized it from the big woman. But the frenzy that had possessed the priestess had grown far worse in Belle-Marie, for she was much more wanton, more mercilessly certain of herself, in her voluptuous posturing.

In her whirling dance, she passed close to the cage that held the roosters, and at the cackles and flutters of alarm Belle-Marie paused. With a feline grace, she swooped to flip back the lid and grasp one of the helpless birds by the feet. She flung it high, laughing as it squawked and flapped its wings, then she reached down and dragged the knife from its place. She slashed at the cockerel, nearly cutting off a wing. Again and again she flayed him, splitting his breast, gouging feathers and flesh from his legs. Slowly, his white feathers grew red with blood. Blood spattered Belle-Marie's face, her shoulders, and her breasts where her cloth, freed from the knife pinning it in place, was slipping from her body. Then while the cockerel still lived, she flung it spinning through the air to land in the boiling pot on the fire. Stooping, she seized another bird from the cage.

There was an atmosphere of unrestrained violence, of released hate, and of lust growing about the quadroon.

Claire tasted the sickness rising in her throat and turned her head, only to look back again as a great cry rose from the crowd before her.

She saw Belle-Marie, naked, her body dripping with the blood of the decapitated rooster in her left hand, while she drank from a bowl the blood she had drained. The drums pounded as hands began to reach for the new Voodooienne, hands reaching for power, hands reaching in lust, and through the crowd there swept a wave of madness as scratching, biting, and clawing they fell upon each other.

Claire stumbled back, one hand to her mouth. She could not watch. She had to get away. Where was Octavia? She did not dare call to her for fear that the madness in the clearing would reach out and sweep her into it. In which direction had the older woman gone? From which direction had they come? The horrible things she had seen had left her disoriented. But then, as she heard a soft footfall behind her, it ceased to matter. She ran.

Vines and saw briars turned vicious, tore at her hair. Sharp twigs and dead limbs bruised her pounding feet through her thin slippers, while tree roots reached out to trip her. She slipped on the loose leaves that carpeted the ground. A tree branch stung her eye and rasped across her face as she ducked beneath it.

Then from out of the black night behind her there came a whisper of sound past her shoulder. A knife, thrown hard, buried itself with a thud in the great live oak tree ahead of her!

Claire was so startled that she stumbled and fell head-long, catching at the tree for support. Starlight glinted on the blade and gleamed from a hilt that looked like *cloisonné* enamel. She did not wait to be certain. Long before the thought of self-protection had formed in her mind, the hilt was in her hand and she had pulled the blade from the hard, resisting wood.

She turned, at bay, and stood listening, holding her breath that she might hear better. The noise of the voodoo gathering seemed far away, and around her the night stood unnaturally still. Then there came a crackling noise, and Octavia, the wide wings of her peculiar gown rippling around her, broke from the darkness. Claire could not see her face, but her voice held only gentle chiding.

"Claire, my dear girl, whatever came over you?"

Without knowing quite why she did it, Claire let her arm fall so that the knife was hidden among the folds of her skirt.

"That ceremony—it was horrible!" she cried with loathing.

"Yes, I agree. At least, it seems so to our eyes. But one must not judge by our standards."

"Torturing live animals can be nothing but cruel, regardless of the standard you use."

"Don't distress yourself about it, Claire. It has been done so for hundreds of years, and will continue to be done in spite of us."

Claire let it go. "But—what of your cat?"

"Perfectly well. For a price, the priestess forced a concoction down his throat, and the black imp got up and walked off by himself. I have little doubt that we will find him waiting for us on the doorstep when we return."

She proved an able prophet. As they neared the house, the cat came from the darkness to wind himself about their legs. The purring noise in his throat had a rough note, as if he had strained his vocal chords, but otherwise he seemed entirely normal.

Glancing up toward the room she shared with Justin, Claire thought she saw a shadow cross the window. It would be Justin now, surely. What was she to say? Your mistress tried to kill me? She caught the inside of her lip between her teeth, trying to think.

Her action in hiding the knife from Octavia troubled her. And having kept silent before his aunt, could she begin to explain to her husband, the moment she saw him, what had happened? It would seem odd to say the least.

The dagger, it seemed, was an embarrassment she could do without. She had no wish to sow discord between Justin and herself, there was enough between them already. And she was afraid, deathly afraid, that his sympathies would lead him to doubt her word if Belle-Marie chose to deny her story. She did not want a test of strength between herself and Belle-Marie. She knew too well who would win.

And so, as they neared the front steps, Claire stopped. She bent down, as though to tie her slipper, and thrust the dagger beneath a clump of fern.

She would retrieve it in the morning at a time when it would be easier to hide it in her room or some other place about the house. Why she wanted to keep it secreted she did not know, but just then it seemed important.

Justin was standing beside the fireplace, a glass of sherry in his hand, when she stepped through the french door. He raised an eyebrow, his eyes traveling from her disordered hair to her stained slippers. With a leisurely grace, he reached out and pulled the bell rope, summoning Rachel.

"Octavia and I were walking," Claire answered his unspoken query, but avoided his eyes. She unbuttoned her spencer and tossed it onto the bed, then ran a hand over her hair, trying to smooth it back into her slipping chignon.

"It seems to have put color into your cheeks," Justin observed.

Claire felt her face grow warmer, and she glanced at him out of the corner of her eyes. He was dressed for dinner in a coat of claret superfine, a color that went well with his brand of dark, feline looks. The scar, she thought, gave a savage cast to his features and now that the surprise and instinctive horror of its presence had passed, actually added to his appearance.

She had not realized that she was staring at the scar until he turned abruptly away. Then, since Rachel chose that moment to tap on the door, he opened it, and strode from the room.

Could he have thought that her feelings were of repugnance? The thought filled her with such dismay that it was a moment before she could attend to her maid's inquiry and point out the dress she intended to wear for supper.

It was after breakfast the next day before she had the opportunity to retrieve the knife. Every moment until that time someone, it seemed, had been at her side; Justin, Octavia, Helene, or Berthe. At last, in the middle of morning, she contrived to slip away by herself. But even as she knelt and slipped her hand beneath the fern, a voice spoke behind her.

"Found something?"

Shock made her jerk her hand back, her hand with the fingers curled around the blade of the knife.

"Y-yes," she stammered, getting to her feet and turning to face the overseer. What was his name? Ben. That was it.

"It looks to be a knife of some kind," the man said. "Fancy frog-sticker." He stared from her to the knife, his head cocked on one side and both hands on his hips.

The knife was about six inches long with a thin, four-sided blade, a rounded guard, and a hilt of turquoise enamel set in gold tracery.

"It must be valuable," she ventured, turning it in her hand as if she had never seen it before.

"Reminds me of that bunch Edouard's got hanging on his wall. Betcha a Spanish real it'll be one of his."

Memory stirred. She did vaguely recall someone, perhaps Berthe, mentioning that Edouard collected knives. She did not think, however, that this one could be a part of his collection, but she could hardly say so. It was such an obvious possibility, especially to someone who did not know how it came to be lying beneath the fern.

"I will have to ask Edouard about it," she said thoughtfully.

"No need. He's down at the copperage, saw him there myself not more than ten minutes ago. Be glad to take it to him."

"Oh, I wouldn't dream—"

"No trouble," he insisted, holding out his hand, his eyes too bright, too appraising as he stared at her, slowly shifting his wad of chewing tobacco to the far side of his mouth, where it bulged in his cheek as he smiled with yellowed teeth. His shirt showed sweat stains under his arms, and the leather suspenders that held his breeches were twisted and curling at the edges with age. His boots were caked with mud. None of these things would have mattered if there had not been the arrogance in his stance that expected her to overlook them.

Controlling a feeling of distaste, Claire handed him the knife with the hilt toward him, taking care that their fingers did not touch. With a murmured thank you she turned and left him, but as she looked back he was still standing, following her with his eyes. He was no longer smiling.

She had almost reached her room before it occurred to her that now, with the knife gone from her possession, there was no way for her to prove what had happened in the swamp if she tried to tell of it. Ben had wanted the quadroon girl. Suppose they were lovers? Belle-Marie might have sent him to bring back the knife. Had he stared at her in such a manner because he knew the quadroon had tried to kill her, and that she was too unsure of herself to admit it? Or was it some more personal inclination that filled his mind? Shuddering a little, she could not help glancing once more over her shoulder. Ben was walking away toward the trail that led to the swamp. The person hastening to meet him was not the quadroon, however. It was Edouard.

A terrible doubt gripped her as she watched them meet, saw the knife change hands, and then the two men walking off together. They were probably doing nothing more than holding a discussion about some phase of plantation work, she tried to tell herself. She was becoming suspicious of everyone and it was too easy to see conspiracy everywhere. But it was odd to see Edouard around the house at that time of the day.

She turned toward her room, then stopped with a gasp of surprise. Justin stood in the door, a look of such blackness on his face that she almost took a step backward.

"Is—is something wrong?" she asked.

"With a woman one never knows."

"I don't know what you mean," she said, but because of what she had kept from him, a guilty flush crept to her hairline.

His eyes narrowed as he gazed down at her and the scar on his face seemed to stand out in a ridge. "You are my wife. I would advise you not to forget it."

"I am not likely to do so," she said, seeing at last that he was referring to her obvious interest in the two men. Perhaps he had even seen her talking to Ben a few moments ago.

Justin stepped back, and with her head high Claire made to brush past him. But he grasped her arm, his fingers bruising her flesh so that she bit back a cry of pain.

"Don't try my patience, Claire. When it snaps I might enjoy the consequences. You, I'm persuaded, would not!"

Chapter Eight

SHE WAS HUNGRY for the first time in weeks. Since the evening before, when she had seen the cat become so ill after eating her meal, she had not eaten alone. Breakfast she had eaten in the dining room with the others. She had not dared to comment, even to Octavia again, about the possibility that she had slowly been poisoned, but she was growing hourly more certain that such had been the case. Her increasing appetite, her general sense of renewed well-being, seemed to prove it. She refused to think of how it might have been done, and yet now she drank nothing, ate nothing, that either Rachel or Justin's man brought to the room, unless it was also to be shared by her husband. She felt certain Belle-Marie would not chance harming him.

She had not seen Justin since their confrontation earlier. Which meant that though it was late, nearly time for the noon meal, nothing had passed her lips. She had missed the eleven o'clock coffee

137

and cakes she usually enjoyed. If she waited until Justin had also changed clothes for dinner, he might suggest ordering a carafe of fresh water at least, but she could not wait. She did not wish to see him alone. His threat, veiled though it had been, was too fresh in her mind. Even the memory of it made her clench her hands to still their trembling.

Jumping up from her chair, she stood in the center of the floor as she heard footsteps approaching along the gallery. Then as her nerve deserted her, she fled to Octavia's room.

Octavia was not there. More than likely she was in the kitchen with the cook or supervising the laying of the table for dinner. Claire stood listening, but she could hear no sound from the dining room. The house was quiet with the somnolence of a warm summer's day. The blinds were closed, shutting out the hot brilliance of the sun, leaving the rooms in semidarkness. For a moment it seemed to Claire that she was alone in the house, free of constraint, free to be herself; then a door slammed somewhere toward the back. She moved toward the door connecting Octavia's room with the dining room, expecting to see the older woman appear on her way back from the outside kitchen. Still she did not come.

But as Claire swung from the open door, she noticed that another of the four doors from Octavia's room stood open a thin crack. The room beyond was the bedroom in the front of the house, Edouard's room, she was almost positive.

From where she stood she could see the head of the bed with its posts holding a high tester, and a portion of a table holding a whale-lamp of pewter. The thought of the knife collection Ben had mentioned stirred, and almost without realizing what she was doing she moved to touch the door, making it swing noiselessly inward. She stood still a moment, listening, her gaze fastened on the wall of knives around the head of the bed. When she was sure the room was unoccupied, she stepped inside.

There were small, thin daggers, to fit the hand of a woman, slender stilettos, and also wider, more dangerous looking blades, blades as short as three inches, and those that came close to being swords. Some were bare, while others were sheathed in scabbards of intricate workmanship, chased, carved, or inlaid with gold, ivory, or wood set with semi-precious stones.

Claire let her gaze roam the wall until she found what she sought, a bare hook with a light shadow on the wallpaper in the thin shape of a knife. She had reached up to trace the outline with the tip of her finger when there was a slight sound behind her.

"What are you doing in here?"

Claire froze, her breath catching in her throat. Then she swung slowly around to face the woman who stood in the door leading from the gallery. Her mind felt numb, but as she saw who it was she swallowed and managed a smile.

"Why, Berthe, you startled me. I—I was going to the dining room when your son's collection of knives caught my eye. You don't think he will mind if I admire them?"

Berthe did not answer that directly. She moved slowly into the room. "You are thinking, I don't doubt, that Edouard gets his hoarding instinct from me. Oh, you needn't deny it. It has often been remarked upon. We are not a family who easily gives up anything we have ever owned. We enjoy the mere fact of possession, a trait not to be wondered at, I think, when we have always been dependent for the necessities of life on someone else, first my husband's brother, and now, his son." Her voice was quiet, her pallid face without expression, and yet there was an intensity about her. Was it always there, Claire wondered? Perhaps it was the contrast with the vivid Helene that had made Berthe appear such a mousey creature.

"But are you interested in knives? My husband began this collection many years ago, and my son has added to it. Let me see if I can remember for you, and tell you a little about them. Some of them are extremely old; one or two are more than three hundred years in age. This one, for instance, is called a *cinquedea*. See the broad, tapering blade? It is almost a sword, isn't it? And here is the kidney dagger, an illustrative name, don't you think? There are one or two left handed knives, for use when a sword was held in the right hand during a fight or duel, and you see several with unusual guards to protect the hands and fingers. Some are very pretty things, I think, with the gold and jewels and the chasing on the blades. But you must ask Edouard about them. He can tell you so much more than I."

"Oh, I felt only the most idle curiosity," Claire declared, trying for a light laugh. "A knife is not a woman's weapon."

"I expect you are right. The thought offends, does

it not? So physical. But come, let us go into the dining room. Octavia will be annoyed if we are late for dinner." Berthe turned toward the gallery door through which she had entered.

"Could we go this way?" Claire asked, indicating the direction of Octavia's room. "The sun is so hot on the gallery floor that it burns through my slippers."

"Yes, of course, I quite understand, my dear. I remember when I was carrying Edouard, the heat affected me in much the same way."

"Oh, but—"

"You must not be embarrassed. You will have to get used to comments. Octavia, I am sure, will not spare your blushes, nor will Helene, when you begin to lose your shape. Helene can be quite vicious. She considers all other women as rivals in some vast competition, I think. She is not a happy woman. I have always been glad she was not here to torment me while I was *enciente*. My son, you know, is older than Justin."

"Yes, so I understand," Claire said, as they moved through the door into the dining room. She was happy to have the subject of her supposed pregnancy passed over.

"Her vanity would not allow her to be seen while she herself was in a family condition. She actually persuaded Marcel to carry her abroad."

"Pride is a strange thing," Claire commented as Berthe paused expectantly.

"Indeed so. I am glad that beauty has never been a consideration with me. My son is my pride."

"I'm sure such a sentiment will give you more

joy," Claire managed to comment after casting about in her mind for a response.

Berthe nodded. "My son has never caused me the least concern—well, I cannot truly say that. There was once, but I'm sure it was nothing to signify."

"You mean the scar, I think."

"Yes, you are so very understanding. I hope you will not hold it against Edouard. I'm sure he never meant to do it. It was only a thoughtless child's prank."

Perhaps it was natural for her to defend her son, Claire told herself, but a feeling of anger shook her at the woman's dismissing tone, as though it was unimportant that Justin had been left with a scarred face as a constant reminder of the incident.

Dinner was a strained occasion. Flies buzzed over the bowls and platters, only barely discouraged by the *chasses mouches*, or ceiling fan, that creaked overhead. The boy, seated in the doorway, whose job it was to pull the rope that set the contraption to swaying, was half asleep with the warmth and the monotony of the task. Now and then Octavia would clear her throat and fix him with her dark gaze as a hint that he should bestir himself.

Octavia seemed to have her mind on other things, however, for when not seeing to the table service, she lapsed into a grim abstraction. It was left to Berthe to try to make conversation, supported by her son, until Helene, with a twisted smile and a glance around the table, informed her that she was wasting her time.

"Oh? But I have nothing but time," Berthe said softly. "Widows only mark time until death takes them to dwell with their loved ones."

"Spare us. We have all heard of your bereavement until we are weary of it, and today my nerves will not bear any more," Helene said, staring at the opposite wall over the heads of the others.

"Helene, Berthe, please—" Octavia said, as if suddenly aware of the tension around her.

"But don't you agree, Octavia?" Berthe insisted. "We three, you, Helene, and I, are all waiting for the release of death?"

"I don't like this conversation. Please let us speak of something else."

"Even those who are dearest to us in the next generation cannot make up for the ones we have lost, don't you find? One's own son is little consolation. You understand, I know, Octavia," she smiled, her eyes bright with watchfulness.

Claire was startled to see the color drain from Octavia's face. And as she turned to Berthe, she thought she saw a faint smile just disappearing from her mouth. What could the woman mean? Octavia had no son. Why should she understand more readily than Helene? Claire recognized that a part of Berthe's insinuations might concern Helene's mourning for Gerard, but it seemed unlikely that she would mention it publicly, even by intimation. Perhaps, then, she had meant to compare Helene's state, as the wife of a man totally paralyzed, to widowhood? She sighed. She did not understand the innuendoes she could sense below the surface of the exchange between the two women. She was relieved when Edouard cleared his throat and engaged her in reminiscence of New Orleans.

She ate conscientiously, knowing she needed to regain her strength, but in that atmosphere of strain she rapidly lost her appetite. It did not help that every time she looked up she found her husband watching her, an inscrutable expression on his face. She felt a certain guilty gladness when, after the meal, Justin elected to return to the fields and she could escape to the privacy of her room to rest, alone with her thoughts.

She slept heavily, awakening with a feeling of depression. A tired staleness hung over her, and she stared at the walls, trying to gather the vitality it would take to get up. It was only the thought of a cooling sponge bath that made the effort possible.

It was still some time before the supper bell would ring, but dressing would take up time, and so she allowed Rachel to slip a dress of plum gauze trimmed with gold ribbons over her head. Then she sat fanning, trying to keep her hair from sticking to her perspiration-damp face, while the maid arranged her hair.

She had not realized that the fan she was using was the one Justin had presented to her in her wedding basket until he stepped into the room and stood for a moment with his eyes fixed upon it.

Claire gave him a hesitant smile in the mirror, but he did not return it. He looked away, then crossed to a chair and sat down with his legs stretched out before him. Staring at nothing, he pulled his shirt from his pants and stripped it off, dropping it in a heap on the floor.

Claire colored a little as she looked quickly away from his broad shoulders and the gold medal on a chain that glittered against the bronze skin of his chest.

"It is very hot," she said, irritated that her voice came out with such a breathless quality.

"It is, which leads me to wonder for whom you are expending all this energy prinking yourself?"

"Why, for myself, I suppose."

"Are you certain? Edouard was most attentive at dinner."

"Was he? I'm sure I did not notice."

"I'm sure you did."

Claire compressed her lips, but she did not answer, for while it might have been true that Edouard had held her chair and made an effort to interest her in several of the dishes, she knew his motive had been merely to ease the tension and make her feel welcome.

"I don't believe I have seen that dress."

"Perhaps not, but it is a part of my trousseau."

"Why haven't I?"

"It—seemed more suitable for this kind of weather. It is rather—" she touched the low bodice self-consciously.

"I noticed as much," he observed with a dry note in his voice.

Claire glanced at Rachel's impassive face. The maid, intent on winding a curl around her finger, seemed to be deaf to their conversation, but Claire could not disregard her presence. She sent Justin a warning look.

He smiled without humor. "Rachel, be so good as to pull the bell for me," he directed. "I feel the need of a bath."

As the girl obeyed, Claire cast about in her mind for an excuse to leave him alone without appearing routed.

Justin's valet appeared and was given his instructions. Then as Rachel patted the last pin and the last curl into place, Claire rose to her feet.

"The sun is down now. I think I will see if it is cooler on the gallery."

"It will be, I'm sure," Justin said smoothly, the gleam in his eyes informing her that he was not fooled by her maneuver. She considered staying just to see what he would do, but as he removed his boots with the help of his valet, and then began to slide his suspenders from his shoulders, Claire dismissed the idea as foolish in the extreme. But that did not keep her from chiding herself for cowardice as she dismissed her maid and left him.

The evening was still; the light limpid, drenched with dew. Mosquito hawks made buzzing silhouettes against the orchid-blue sky. The scent of flowers hung in the air. The sound of her own footsteps were loud in Claire's ears, a disturbance in the peaceful quiet, so that as she reached the front steps she descended to walk on the grass. Her slippers, the hem of her gown, were soon wet with dew, but she did not mind. At least she was away from the house, away from being watched, weighed, and found wanting.

Now why had that thought struck her? It was Justin who most often watched her, and why should it matter that he found her disappointing?

Before she could pursue the thought, a flicker of movement caught her eye and she looked back toward the house. Around the corner, from the back garden, there came a woman dressed in white, her skirts fluttering about her and her head covered with a white kerchief. In her hands she carried a large crystal vase filled with a mass of full-blown white roses. The woman stared straight ahead, walking with an unseeing stare.

"Helene."

In that startled moment of recognition, Claire said the name aloud, but if Justin's mother heard, she made no sign. She went on walking toward the path that led a short distance away on this side of the house, the opposite side from the swamp, toward a slight rise surrounded by a stand of cedar trees, those somber, black-green trees of mourning casting their shade over the marble tombs of the family cemetery.

The woman in white mounted the rise and stood beside a grave, its tomb sitting above the ground as was the custom in this swampy country, where a grave filled with seeping water before the coffin could be lowered. The vase she sat on top of the marble, then she dropped to her knees and rested her head against it with her hands clutching the sides. Even at that distance the low moaning sound could be heard, the sound of pain, or grief.

Claire followed Helene for a few steps, wondering if there were not something she could say or do to alleviate that terrible grief. Then as that sound went on and on and Helene's head rolled back and forth on her shoulders, she stopped. She could not interfere. There was nothing that could be done to ease such a personal torment.

But she could not leave. The evening sky turned to purple and the nightbirds began to cry and still she stayed. She could not say quite what held her there; a vulgar curiosity, a desire to be of service if she was needed, or simply the half formed intention to protect Helene from interruption and the embarrassment of prying eyes. When at last Justin's mother dragged herself to her feet, Claire stepped back out of sight, looking away from the tear-ravaged face as the woman walked by.

When she was gone, Claire climbed slowly up the incline and under the cedars until she had reached the tomb over which Helene had wept. She was not surprised when she read the name chiseled into the marble. It was the tomb of Gerard. Gerard, her husband's brother.

And so Helene had loved him. They had lived together at Sans Songe, loving each other, perhaps, beneath the eyes of his wife, her husband, their children. Had they met clandestinely in the swamp? Had it come to that? And had her son discovered them, demanded satisfaction, and killed Gerard before his mother's eyes? Could that be why the duel was said to be an odd affair? And was that why Helene hated her son, because he had killed the man she loved?

Who was at fault? Justin, for resorting to a brand of civilized murder, or Helene for her infidelity? Gerard for sinning against his brother, or Marcel for being unable to hold his wife? Or was the true villain the custom of the *mariage de convenance*, that loveless bond between two people?

The thought struck home and she flinched, seeing in her mind's eye the barren future that stretched before her. Would she some day carry roses to a grave because she had reached out for a love denied her within the bonds of matrimony? Desolation settled over her shoulders, then it was replaced by an invading fear. If her husband had taken such a reprisal for the sake of his father's honor, what would he not do for his own? What form might his revenge take if he thought his wife had played him false? Remembering his anger, his threatening tone earlier that morning, Claire shivered.

Suddenly there was a touch on her arm. As warm fingers closed over it, she flinched, and there was a lurking fright in her eyes as she swung around to face her husband.

"What are you doing here?" he grated, with a glance at the tomb beside them.

"N-nothing. Just walking," she answered, too unsure, too ashamed, to admit that she had followed Helene.

"I cannot bear a liar. You were exercising your curiosity, weren't you? Berthe told me you were fascinated by the portrait of Gerard. Even in death he is irresistible." There was a vicious sarcasm in his voice.

"No, it wasn't like that," she protested, confusion and a haunting distrust lending desperation to her voice.

He stared at her, the scar standing out on his set face. Unconsciously, his fingers tightened, and Claire's lips parted in a silent protest at the pain, though she did not dare move.

"What is it, Claire? Why do you look at me so?"

"Please," she whispered.

"You would like to get away, wouldn't you? You can't bear my house, my family—or me."

"I—"

"Don't bother to deny it. Your actions betray you.

You shrink when I come near, you flinch at my touch. I warn you. You will never get away from me. The sooner you resign yourself, the better for you."

For a moment longer his eyes held hers, then his lips descended, hard, demanding a response, if nothing more than surrender. She was crushed against him, held in an inescapable bondage. He kissed the corners of her trembling mouth, her eyelids, the curve of her cheeks, and the tender softness of her neck. She was acutely aware of his touch, his caresses, and yet her mind felt adrift. Liquid fire ran through her veins, and it seemed that to match his passion with equal ardor was the only way to avoid total capitulation.

At last he raised his head. As Claire saw the glitter of triumph in his eyes, she knew that he was exulting in his mastery. Suffocation gripped her throat and tears rose to her eyes. She clenched her teeth, fighting to control her voice. "I hope that was—satisfactory."

His smile faded and a gray look crept over his face. He let her go abruptly, and she stumbled back.

"Damn you," he said with a low intensity, then turning on his boot heel, he strode away.

Claire watched him until he was hidden by the trees and the walls of the house. On her lips the impression of his kiss still burned. She felt no sense of victory, only a strange ache of regret. She took a long, deep breath and let it out on a shuddering sigh, then began slowly to follow him back to the house.

* * *

Justin did not appear at the supper table, though Claire was certain that that had been his intention. When the meal was over and they all sat over their coffee in the salon, Edouard took the place beside her and thanked her for the return of his knife.

"Ben said you found it. I can't imagine how it came to be outside. I hesitate to blame the servants, though I expect my collection is a serious temptation. In fact Octavia often tells me that I'll wind up one day with my throat cut. She thinks all knives should be locked away in a household like this."

"Yes, my aunt used to lock the cutlery away in a special mahogany knife box each evening," Claire said, all the while wondering cynically if what she was hearing was a fabrication. Was his voice too casual, his manner too offhand? If his daggers were so precious why, indeed, hadn't he taken more care of them?

"The dagger that was missing was a *quillon* dagger, not as valuable as some, but I suppose the bright hilt made it irresistible."

But if Edouard's supposition was not correct, what was the explanation? How had the dagger come into Belle-Marie's possession? Could the quadroon woman have entered the house without anyone being aware of it? She was not a ghost or a spirit, to flit about unseen, and yet somehow she had managed to leave the voodoo *gris-gris* for Claire to find, both in New Orleans and here at Sans Songe.

"You have a great number of knives. You must have been collecting for some time."

"Actually, my father began it, but I found it interesting enough to continue. You acquire a bit of history with each knife. The Spaniard with his beard and ruff and his poniard, the helmeted crusader knight bearing home the crescent-shaped Arabic dagger as a prize." He shrugged. "It appeals to me."

"And do you collect the tales of murder done with each blade?" The question rose to her lips before she was aware of it forming in her mind.

An arrested look came over his face, a look of withdrawal, then he laughed. "You can't be serious."

She shook her head, smiling to convince him she was merely being flippant, suddenly losing the courage to continue.

"What are you two talking about with your heads together?" Octavia asked, plumping herself down beside Edouard.

"My knife collection, for the most part."

"Ah yes, the *quillon* dagger is missing, isn't it? I noticed as much yesterday evening when I saw to the changing of the linens. You have found it?"

"Yes, Claire and Ben found it on the walk, and he handed it back to me."

"Obliging of him."

It had been obliging, Claire thought, but the man had been almost too anxious to see the knife back in Edouard's hands. Why? What did he hope to gain?

As if in echo of her own thoughts, she heard Octavia say, "I would watch that Ben. He strikes me as one who never does anything without some idea of repayment."

"A trusting thing, aren't you?" Edouard teased her.

She pulled the skirts of her tent of a costume, this evening in blending shades of yellow, about her. "I've learned to trust few and love fewer. It is less painful that way."

Claire lay thinking later of Octavia and of what she had said. Most emotion, it seemed—whether trust, love, hate, or fear—brought little but pain. But that was living, and there was little to do but accept it, to take what happiness was offered, and not look beyond.

But happiness seemed an ephemeral thing, existing on another plane, vaguely remembered, but without the possibility of attainment.

Justin had not come home. In the glow of the moonlight she could see the sheets of his day bed stretched fresh and smooth. Where was he? Was he with Belle-Marie in some primitive cabin in the swamp?

She shook her head, retreating from the image she had conjured up in her mind.

She could remember in such detail what had happened that afternoon, the feel of his lips on hers, the roughness of his coat beneath her fingers. To think of him holding another woman with the same strength, the same possessiveness, brought the tightness of mingled rage and pain to her chest.

But she could not be jealous. Jealousy stemmed from love. And she could not love the man who had forced this marriage upon her for some peculiar whim of pride and vanity. The man who neglected her for the company of his quadroon mistress, and who appeared not to care whether she lived or died so long as she did not succeed in defying him or resisting his physical persuasion. A man who had committed murder, the murder of his uncle.

How could she love a man like that, she demanded in self-disgust as tears trailed from the corners of her eyes and soaked into her pillow.

How could she?

Chapter Nine

CLAIRE SAT ON the bed staring at the wall. She was dressed, her hair done. It was morning, the sun shone brightly through the windows. But an aimless feeling possessed her. Without Justin and his valet to enliven the time of rising, the day seemed flat. She was aware of a vague desire to cry. What she needed was something to do, something to divert her thoughts, but there was nothing.

Rachel fussed about the room, gathering up a few articles to be washed, making the four-poster bed, twisting the hair from the brush and putting it into Claire's combing box. It seemed somehow strange to think of the years stretching ahead when, during her old age, she would appreciate having those combings to supplement her own hair. Would she still be waiting then for Justin to come from his mistress?

"Is there anything else you wish to be laundered, madame?" The maid's words broke her absorption.

"No, I don't suppose, Rachel, not if Monsieur Justin's man has taken his master's clothes."

"Then if you do not require me, I will attend to these."

Claire nodded absently, and the maid slipped from the room after a hurried curtsey. She had been gone only a few minutes when a tap came on the door.

"Moping?" Octavia asked, as she entered the room without ceremony.

"No, of course not," Claire answered, unreasonably annoyed. "Why should you think so?"

"The length of your face. And the fact—conveyed unerringly by the servant grapevine—that Justin was absent last night."

"And—does the grapevine say where he was?"

She shrugged. "There are several opinions, none of which should concern you. The only explanation that can, or should, be of interest is your husband's, when he comes home. Don't you agree?"

"I suppose."

"Aren't you sure? Is the esteem in which you hold him so low that you don't wish to hear from his own lips where he has been?"

"Justin, you must know, is not given to explaining his actions. And in any case, I'm not sure I want to hear him admit where he has been. Surely you haven't forgotten Belle-Marie, Octavia?"

"Hardly, but, Claire, theirs was not the kind of relationship that endures. I do not believe that Justin encouraged his *chère-aime* to follow him. Some men, it is true, maintain two households after marriage, they cleave to their quadroons and see to the welfare and education of the children born of the union, just as they do for their legitimate offspring. But Justin has no children of Belle-Marie. The woman has no hold on him, not even of the senses; at least, none that you need fear."

Claire, staring down at her hands, did not answer. Octavia did not understand and she could not bring herself to explain.

"Oh, I know what you are thinking. You say to yourself, she knows nothing of love and misunderstanding. Don't trouble to deny it, I can see it in your eyes. But you are wrong. I was in love once, years ago. He was an *émigré*, of good family, a *comte*. There were many such in exile from France during the revolution. So long ago, more than thirty years." She sighed.

"And—what happened?"

"We had an idyllic summer. The banns were being read for the second week, my wedding gown was almost ready. There had been yellow fever in New Orleans for a week, but we were too happy to take account of it, or of the fact that it is particularly dangerous for those who are new to our climate. Then my Étienne sickened. He lay ill for several days, fighting to stay alive, fighting for our happiness. Then he died, the day before our wedding day. Once, in his delirium, he begged me to go for the priest so that he might marry us before the end, but I was so certain Étienne would live. He was so strong, so vital, it was impossible that he could die. I have often regretted—ah, but it is vain. Regret helps nothing."

There was an old sorrow in her voice, a dry pain brought back across the years and made to live.

Why? Puzzlement as well as compassion must have shown in her face, for Octavia went on.

"I tell you this because I know how important it is for two people who are in love to share their fears and worries. I have this feeling that there is something terribly wrong between you and Justin. I'm not so certain what it is—and certainly it is none of my business. I know that, and I will not pry into the affair. But let me urge you, Claire, not to let pride stand in the way of your happiness. Women you know, are not bound by the same kind of honor as men. It is no disgrace to show a little weakness or need, as it is for a man. Anger and righteousness worn like banners flying in the wind, the high held head, are no substitute for love and the warmth of belonging."

"Oh, Octavia, you don't know." It was a cry of hurt, coming on her discovery of the night before.

"I said I would not interfere," the older woman began, putting out her hand to pat Claire's that lay clenched in her lap, "but, I don't believe Justin goes to Belle-Marie. Why should he, when he has a beautiful wife like you?"

There was no answer to that. However well meant Octavia's comment had been, she did not understand. Claire looked away at the glow of the sun beyond the gauze curtains at the windows.

"Well. I must run along. Forgive me if I have pushed my way in where I had no business. I have grown fond of you, and I don't like to see you unhappy. Or Justin, who has always been dear to me."

Claire managed to smile and shake her head as Octavia got to her feet and started toward the door.

"Octavia?"

"Yes?" The older woman swung back.

"I am so tired of sitting with nothing to do. Couldn't I help you? There must be something I could do."

There was a slight pause as the door behind Octavia opened and Rachel stepped into the room. The girl murmured an apology as she nearly collided with Octavia. "Excuse me, please, I did not mean to bother you, but I just this moment thought of Madame Claire's silk stockings. I left them in the armoire, and I felt sure she would wish them to be rinsed also."

"Get on with it then, girl," Octavia said, stepping out of the way.

"Yes, of course, Claire. If you really want to help I will find something light for you to do. Just now I think if you truly would like to help, it would be a relief to me if you would go out and sit with Marcel. You need not try to entertain him, he doesn't wish anyone to feel that is necessary. Just bear him company."

"I will be happy to do that," she agreed, "but I would like to do something a bit more active. I was never used to being so quiet, you know, while I lived with my aunt and uncle."

"I won't forget," Octavia promised. "There is plenty on the plantation for willing hands." Then, with a smile, she went sweeping away about her business.

It was peaceful on the loggia. The sun inched slowly in toward them, pushing the shade back bit by bit. Sparrows flitted about the eaves where they had built a nest, and a blue-jay hopped about the steps. The cries of the other birds hidden in the trees beyond the limits of the garden came to them. Now and then a breeze stirred the air, fluttering the pages of the sketchbook in Claire's lap.

For amusement, Claire sketched the jay with his head cocked inquisitively, eyeing them, then she did a quick view of the garden with its geometric rows of clipped hedge, the fountain bubbling, catching the glitter of the sun, and the sparrows bathing at the shallow edge.

"You are good, madame, very good. The drawing of the garden done in color would be good enough to grace the salon," Anatole told her.

Claire thanked him, noticing the slight nod from Marcel that indicated that his servant had expressed his master's views once again.

Smiling a little, Claire did a rapid sketch of Anatole and presented it to him, happy with the satisfaction she saw on the thin face.

The three of them were quiet after that. The sun was making itself felt as it lingered overhead. The scents drifting to them from the kitchen told them it could not be long until the dinner hour.

Claire doodled idly on her pad, wondering if Justin would be home for dinner, wondering if Marcel knew his whereabouts, if he knew what went on in the house, and what he thought of it. She thought of what she knew of Helene's love for Marcel's brother, and she considered the possibility that all those years before, Marcel had discovered it, and if the fact might not be responsible in some way for the stroke that had left him an invalid.

Suddenly, a sound came from the man beside her, an inarticulate croak of distress. Startled, Claire swung toward Marcel, instinctively reaching out toward him to touch his hands that hung so lifeless. They were trembling.

His chest heaved with the effort of his breathing, and an alarming flush stained the cheeks of his waxen, pale face, His mouth was open to emit the sound he was trying so desperately to form into words.

"Once more he is trying to tell us this thing he has in his mind," Anatole said, his own face contorted as he dropped to one knee beside Marcel's chair.

"Oh, what is it?" Claire cried. Marcel seemed in such a strained agony of effort.

Then together she and Anatole followed Marcel's gaze to the sketchbook that lay forgotten on her lap. He was staring at something she had drawn there, a face frozen in stillness. In her concentration she had sketched the death mask of Gerard.

Her eyes met those of Anatole, then she stared in guilty dismay at Marcel. What a fool she was. She would not have upset him for the world if she could have kept from it. Her eyes filled with tears of distress as she gazed at his straining face, the desperate appeal in his eyes for understanding.

Then came a faint shake of his head.

"He says no," Anatole whispered.

But what was he denying? The question must have shown on her face, for Marcel strained only a moment longer, then he relaxed in his chair. Resignation closed over his face and he let his eyelids fall.

Anatole sighed and slowly got to his feet. "I am sorry, Madame Claire. You—must not blame yourself."

She looked away, blinking back tears, brushing at those that spilled down her cheeks. It was ridiculous that she should cry, but she could not help it. Tears were so close to the surface these days.

"My master will be tired—" Anatole suggested tentatively.

"Yes, I had better wash for dinner, too," Claire said, hastily getting to her feet, hugging the offending pad to her chest. Anatole, she knew, did not like to have anyone watch him at the difficult business of maneuvering Marcel back to his room that opened out onto the loggia.

"Monsieur Leroux—Father Leroux," she said softly. "I am so sorry. I will see you this afternoon."

She was rewarded by the faint twitch of the lips that signified a smile. Turning, she went quickly into the house.

Justin was not in the house when the dinner bell rang, but halfway through the meal they were startled by the sudden jangle of his bell from the loggia as he rang for his valet. Though she had not been aware of an anxiety for his safety, Claire felt relief wash over her. She glanced at Octavia with a half smile, then looked away from the understanding and gladness she saw in the other woman's hazel eyes.

Claire did not go at once to her bedroom. She wandered out onto the shady front gallery to give Justin time to change his clothes. It was there that Rachel found her.

"Pardon, Madame Claire. Mam'zelle Octavia wishes you to come to her in the quarters. She needs your help with a child who has cut himself on a cane knife."

"Thank you. I'll be glad to come, but I am not sure of my direction."

"I am to take you to her," the girl said, bowing her head as she let her eyelids fall, and turned away.

Happy to be taken at her word and even happier to put off the meeting with Justin, Claire moved forward. She could not think just yet how she should behave toward her husband.

She went with Rachel down the front stairs and around the house to the left. There they took a beaten path through a hedge past the carriage house to a double row of small houses standing on each side of a street. Chickens scratched in the dust of the small front yards, and behind each house was a small garden plot. A whitewashed chapel sat at the end of the street, while nearby was a large building with a shaded front porch. On the porch, several older women sat rocking, the nursemaids for the children who peered from the doors, children whose mothers were at work about the plantation. A sultry quiet hung over the quarters, the quiet of a hot summer afternoon. There was no sign of Octavia.

"In here," Rachel directed her softly, leading the way toward the house on the near end standing with its door open. She stepped aside at the entrance for Claire to precede her.

It was dark inside the room, in contrast to the bright sun outside, and she stood still for a moment. Then, suddenly, there was a scraping sound behind her, and the door slammed shut!

She whirled around, more in surprise than in

fear, and then she heard the solid clunk of a wooden bar being dropped into place.

"Rachel!" she called to the girl, a rising note in her voice. She gave a little push on the door. It would not budge.

"Rachel!" she called again in sudden wrath. "Let me out at once!"

But there was no sound from the other side of the thick panel.

As her eyes adjusted to the gloom, Claire looked around. The building had only a single room, a bare room with nothing but a pallet of twisted quilts in one corner, and two small high windows set with bars.

Bars? With a feeling of horror she recognized the building in which she had been locked away. It was the plantation jail.

For a long, terrible moment she considered the possibility that she had been locked in on the orders of the master of Sans Songe, Justin. Then she thought of Belle-Marie, and was so glad that she had, that she felt weak.

But why would Rachel do the quadroon's bidding? She remembered the tight, shut-in look that came at times to her maid's face, the *gris-gris* that had found its way into her room. It occurred to her that perhaps Rachel was afraid, afraid of the power of the voodoo. As she stood there she thought too of the lassitude, the weakness she had had after that *gris-gris* had appeared, and the sickness that had overtaken the cat after it had shared her meal and brought another *gris-gris* to her around its neck. She had not been ill since she had started to take her meals with the family. Who was better to poison her food than Rachel? It must have been she.

In her agitation, she began to pace, striding up and down the tiny room. Then she stood still, staring at the dust motes turning in the light from the high window, stirred by her movements. But why this? Why shut her up in the jail? It was too public. A half dozen people on the street, the old ladies rocking at the nursery, must have seen her shut in here.

Then why weren't they rushing to let her out? There could be no question in their minds about her belonging where she was. She was Madame Claire Leroux, the mistress of the big house! Who would dare to sit back and fail to help her?

A fearful anger lent strength to her arms as she beat against the door calling again and again. "Let me out! Let me out!"

No one came. What—or whom—did they fear that they would not come to her aid?

Time crept. The heat grew intense in the tiny, closed building with the sun beating against it. And as the heat grew, the fetid odor of despair seemed to come from the walls. Like an old man, the sun climbed slowly down from the sky. The evening shadows lengthened until the shade of the tree crept over the jail, bringing coolness with it. Flies buzzed around Claire's face, a curiously drowsy sound, so that once or twice as she sat on the pallet with her back propped against the wall, she found herself dozing. After the first hour she had stopped pounding on the door, ceased calling. It might be best, she thought, not to draw attention to herself. Once or twice she had thought she heard voices muttering outside the window. Later she heard the sounds of shouting and laughter as the workers came in from the fields. Still, nothing happened. She was forgotten, she thought, and was not certain whether to be glad or sorry for it.

It was dark when the bar was lifted and the door pulled open. A man stood silhouetted against the night. Claire got to her feet and stood still against the wall.

"Madame Claire?" the man said, as if he did not immediately perceive her there in the dark.

"Anatole," she whispered, starting forward.

"Come, madame. Forgive me for being so late. I would have come sooner if the fools had only told me. Please don't think unkindly of my people. It was ignorance, stupid superstition, they meant you no harm."

He gave her his arm and led her forward, and as reaction set in, she was glad of the support. She stood a moment, breathing in the fresh, untainted air of freedom while she recovered her composure. Then they walked quickly back toward the house. As they went she thought she could feel dozens of eyes watching.

The house sat quiet, undisturbed by her absence of nearly five hours. Did she matter so little, she asked herself staring up at the lamplight that shone from the dining room.

Anatole left her on the loggia. Wearily, Claire pushed through the french windows into the empty room with its table set for supper. Beyond it, the salon was untenanted also. Where could they all be?

Her heels made a hollow sound as she negotiated

the gallery on the way to her bedroom. But there, too, in spite of a lamp left burning on the washstand, she found no one.

Sighing, she moved to wash her hands and face in the water she poured from the ewer beside the lamp. She wanted nothing more than to lie down on her bed and sleep. It was not, she knew, a physical tiredness, it was her emotions that had exhausted her. Perhaps she did not need to appear for dinner, and yet, she was afraid to eat in her own room. Did they all know what had happened to her, or did no one but Anatole realize?

But perhaps she did not need to eat. She was not hungry. She could not face having to explain, she did not want their sympathy. She wanted only to wash away the feel of confinement, to change her clothes, and then to lie quietly until she had decided what she would do. This harassment, these threats to her safety from Belle-Marie could not go on.

Without ringing for assistance, she removed the dress she was wearing, washed, took down her hair and brushed and dressed it, then slipped into her dressing gown.

She had gone to the armoire to find a small bottle of perfume that had been her uncle's wedding gift to her, when she saw a small, folded piece of paper lying on the floor. She picked it up and started to toss it into the washbowl for the servants to dispose of with the dirty water when she saw her name. Smoothing out the note she saw a wild, unformed scrawl. *"My darling Justin,"* it read. *"If you care to see Claire Leroux, née Hauterive, alive again you will come to me at the meeting ground in the swamp.*" It was signed *Yours devotedly, Belle-Marie.*

The meeting ground in the swamp. It could be none other than the place beside the bayou where the voodoo ceremony had been held. Justin was not here now. He must have gone. He had gone thinking she was there and in danger, while all the while she had been almost within calling distance.

She did not understand. Why should the quadroon do such a thing—unless Octavia was right, unless it was the only way she could bring Justin to her side. A savage joy gripped Claire, then her smile of triumph faded. Once Justin was there, what then? Belle-Marie had not scrupled to try to kill her or to heap humiliation upon her. What did she intend to do to Justin if he had put her from him, if he had proven so impervious to her attraction that she had to resort to blackmail? It was a trap, a dangerous trap that he had walked into for her sake.

With the note still in her hand, she moved quickly to Octavia's door, and after a brief knock, pushed into her room. She was certain the other woman would be dressing for supper. But the room was empty. An eerie shiver of fear ran over her.

Edouard was not in his room either, nor were Berthe or Helene. Anatole, she knew, was with Marcel, but she could not disturb him. He was solely responsible for the sick man, and he had already varied his routine once this evening by coming for her. She could not ask him to leave his helpless master alone again, nor could she upset Marcel by telling him why she had need of his servant. And there were none of the other servants she could trust. There was no one, no one but herself.

With her mouth set in a straight line, she hurried back through the house to her room where she dragged on the dress she had so recently discarded. She had no real idea what she intended to do, but it seemed that if she could show Justin that she was alive and unhurt, he would not be forced to accede to the demands of Belle-Marie. That, at least, she could accomplish by herself.

She had slipped her feet into her shoes and had her hand on the doorknob before she thought of the knife. Turning back, she took up her lamp and moved swiftly into Edouard's room. She ran her eyes over the wall of knives, then went still, frowning. The *quillon* dagger was not there. Its space was bare. Had it been stolen again? No matter, any knife would do. Reaching up she took a long, thin blade, similar in design to the dagger she had been seeking. There, in the uncertain light coming from her own room some distance away, there was not enough difference between them to matter. And then a disquieting thought struck her. That night at the voodoo ceremony she had seen the knife Belle-Marie was using only briefly in the firelight. There was nothing to prove that that knife she was using and the knife that had been thrown at her a few minutes later were the same.

In her hand, the knife she held felt cool and hard, a vicious thing, made expressly to penetrate living flesh. She had never hurt anything or anyone in her life. Would she be able to use it if she needed it? Then her grip tightened on the carved metal and she turned away. She would have to, if there were no other choice.

There was no one to see or question her as she made her way through the rooms to the front gallery. In the shadow of the overhanging roof, she hesitated for a few seconds, but it was not because she was irresolute. When she saw no one in the dark of the front lawn, or near the woods, heard nothing, she began to descend the steps.

Chapter Ten

THE GRASS WAS damp with dew under her slippers as she struck out across the lawn. The moon sailing in brightness just above the treetops caught her in its beam, but she had no time to waste in keeping to the shadows. She had no idea what time the note had been sent. Already she might be too late.

A flutter of wings sent her heart into her throat as she flushed a covey of sleepy quail from the high grass where the lawn merged into the woods. Her ankles stung as the rough grass and briars lashed against them, then the darkness of the forest closed around her. Straining her eyes, she could see the dark slash of the bayou, then as she neared the bank, the glitter of the moonlight on the water. This was her guide to the meeting ground, and she turned, following its loops and twists, her feet seeking naturally the path beaten down by animals and the secret nighttime wanderings of those who sought the meeting place lying deep in the swamp.

It was quiet. She could hear the whisper of her skirts brushing the dried and crumbling leaves aside and the beating of her own heart as the blood shuddered along her veins. Mosquitoes sang around her face and she brushed at them with her free hand. She stumbled once over a root, and at her sudden movement, there was a scuttling rush in the darkness. A rabbit, she thought, catching her breath, or an opossum. The urge to turn back caught her unaware and she stopped, glancing back the way she had come and then ahead into the darkness before her. How much farther did she have to go? Not so far. She must be near the halfway point. But what was she thinking of? She could not, she would not, give in to the fear that clamored in her mind. She was not a child, to be frightened by a few odd noises. She forced her stiff limbs to move and then to keep on moving. She must not think. Imagination is the main ingredient of fear, she told herself as she shifted the knife from one hand to the other to wipe the perspiration from her palms.

She should be coming to it soon. Yes, there was the open space among the trees, brighter with the free entry of the moonlight and the thinner undergrowth around the clearing. Her footsteps slowed as she searched the dimness for movement, straining her ears for the sound of voices.

She stopped, letting the night settle around her. Was she too late? Had Justin come and gone? Then a chill touched her. Could it be—was it possible— that it was another hoax?

As the thought entered her mind and settled

coldly there, she heard a low growl in the under-growth off to her left. And then a scream shattered the night!

Claire whirled around. It seemed so near, not more than twenty feet away. The sound had star-tled the night creatures into silence. The crickets had begun to shrill again before she recognized the sound she had heard. It was a panther!

She peered into the dark until her eyes ached. Where was the animal now, what was he doing? Swallowing, she eased back toward the bank of the bayou. It would not do to lose sight of it. She would be hopelessly lost in a matter of minutes.

Suddenly, she trod on something soft, and stum-bled, going to one knee. The hand she stretched out to save herself fell on something cool and smooth, but yielding, like human flesh.

She jerked her hand away, staring with disbelief at the crumpled form beside her. It was a moment before she could see that it was Belle-Marie, her limbs sprawled in the uncaring awkwardness of death, with blood staining the lovely, mocking face.

Reluctantly, Claire touched the still chest. There was not the faintest movement, but with the wide, glazed eyes reflecting the spring moon, she had not expected there to be any. It was a gesture only, a sop for the mind that could not leave even Belle-Marie to the mercy of the night without being cer-tain she no longer lived. The smell of blood, raw and primitive, filled her nostrils, the blood that shone in streaks on that face and wet the side of her dress, mingling with the darkness of the swamp, the odors of mud and decay. Nausea rose in her throat and she held her breath for a moment, fighting it.

The impulse for flight, headlong, heels flying, beat against her nerves and she sat still, trying to quash it before getting slowly to her feet. She did not think the quadroon had been dead long. Though her arms were cool, her chest had been still warm. Who, or what, had done this thing? The dark stranger who had been her husband for more than a month, Justin, who would never allow anyone to blackmail him, or the black panther nearby, now screaming his displeasure to the night sky at being deprived of his prey by her presence?

She could hear the big cat snarling deep in his throat, a vicious sound that rose into another scream. Where was he exactly? It was hard to pinpoint the sound in the dark woods. It seemed to echo and reecho around her.

Involuntarily, her fingers on the knife in her hand tightened. Her eyes searching the undergrowth, she began to back away from the body of Belle-Marie. Half her mind felt numb with a disbelieving horror, but the other half cautioned her to move slowly, to ignore the sound of the great cat, to pretend he was nothing more than a large version of Bast, the house cat that purred on her lap and took fright at the least sign of opposition.

Then she saw him.

The moon slanted across the top of his high-held head with a blue-black sheen and gleamed red in his eyes. He was a huge animal, frozen into immobility, devouring her with his eyes, a tautness in his muscles as he scented the wind.

Don't panic. The words seemed to whisper in her

mind, and as she stared at that black head and wild eyes through the moon-drenched darkness she remembered the night Bast had crept into her room, and the way she had held him off with nothing more than strength of will. Surely this was no different, if she could only hold that burning gaze without flinching, without losing supremacy.

One moment the great cat was there, and the next he was gone, melting into the shadows of the night.

Claire took a step, another, and then she began to run back along the way she had come. Where had the panther gone? Perhaps he was behind her, or keeping pace in the underbrush beside the track. Every shaking leaf and fluttering twig seemed to harbor his slinking form, every rustle to indicate his sinuous, gliding stride.

Somehow the very act of flight increased her panic. The faster she ran, the more distance she put between herself and the dead girl lying on the ground, the more the horror grew. By the time she reached the house and pounded along the gallery, her breath was sobbing in her throat and her lungs burned with a rasping fire.

She thrust the door of her room open and then with a clawing hand slammed it to behind her. She leaned against it; as her strength left her, she slid to her knees, the knife she had clutched so desperately throughout her flight falling from her nerveless fingers. She was weak. But more than that, she knew in a vague, far-off manner that there had been a change inside her. It was as though something had snapped and she was no longer quite the same person as the girl who had gone so willingly with

Rachel to the quarters earlier. All her life she had been sheltered from the harshness of the world or the suspicion of evil. Now she had no protection against it. Its presence had touched her both physically and mentally, and she seemed to have no defense.

She crouched against the door, unable to wipe from her memory the smell of fresh blood or the terrible mutilation of Belle-Marie.

Her hands were trembling and she stared at them dazedly before clenching them together in an attempt to keep them still. Lifting her head, she gazed around the room. She had thought to feel safe here. Somehow she did not. Was there, she wondered, any real safety anywhere?

Across from her was the door into Octavia's room with its silver-plated lock and protruding key. If she could get to it, turn the key, she might regain an illusion of security.

But even as the thought came, the door was pulled open and Justin stepped into the room.

"Claire, what is it?" he exclaimed.

She froze, staring at him, her eyes dark with fright. He wore dark gray, almost black, and his movements seemed to her strained mind to have about them the grace of the panther in the woods. His eyes were narrowed to slits, a frown rippled across his face, and by some strange quirk of the light, the lamp appeared to reflect in his eyes with a red gleam.

As he started toward her, her brain refused to acknowledge why he frightened her, and yet she could not suppress a cry of alarm nor prevent herself from throwing one hand up before her face as if to ward him off. He stopped as if he had run into a brick wall.

They stared at each other, but before Justin could speak again, Octavia swept into the room.

"What's the matter? I thought I heard—why, Claire—" She moved at once to the girl's side, slanting a glance of interrogation at Justin as she passed him. Then, as she knelt to put her arm around Claire, she gasped.

"Blood—there is blood all over the hem of your dress. Are you hurt?"

As she glanced down, Claire saw there was blood on her hands also and she shuddered, staring at them. Then she looked up at Octavia.

"No—no, not me. It's Belle-Marie. She's—dead. There was blood. So much blood. Her eyes—I forgot to close her eyes. The panther will—he will—We have got to do something!" She looked from Octavia to Justin, but as she saw the harsh frown on her husband's face, she looked away again.

"Claire—" Octavia said in the helpless voice of one who cannot understand. Then as Justin moved to help her to her feet, Claire's hands closed spasmodically on Octavia's wrists.

It was useless. Her shrinking did not deter him.

"No—no," she whispered as she felt his hands close beneath her elbows, but she was pulled to her feet.

As she straightened, the knife slipped from where it had dropped among the folds of her skirt. They stared at it, then before she could catch her breath, Justin shook her.

"Where were you?"

"I—first the jail—then—then the swamp—" she

said through trembling lips. "I saw the note—she said—Belle-Marie—" Her face drained of color as the memory of what she had seen and endured swept in upon her again. Her eyes, pleading for understanding, searched his face. She could not seem to control the words she needed to explain. She knew she was making no real sense, and yet she was powerless to do anything about it. But seeing the incomprehension on Justin's face she tried again.

"The jail—I was in the jail—ask Rachel. She knows."

There was a faint rustle at the door and Rachel coughed, a small, polite sound. "I am sorry, Monsieur Justin. I know nothing of what she is saying. Madame was here in this room all the afternoon, until the time for me to leave after madame was dressed for supper. She told me not to return later to put her in bed, but I saw her run from the woods and I thought she might need me."

For a moment, shock struck through Claire's confusion. "She is lying! She was the one who shut me up in the jail in the quarters. She told me Octavia was inside, and when I went in she closed the door!"

Rachel shook her head slowly as she bit her lip, her eyes never leaving Claire's face.

"But you did! The women saw you. The women on the porch—of the nursery."

She turned to Justin. "Ask them, they will tell you—or Anatole. Ask Anatole. He was the one who let me out."

Justin stared at Rachel. The girl's eyes seemed to hold nothing but sadness.

"No, Monsieur. No. Madame was here. I promise you."

Justin shook his head, his face grave. "I cannot believe that Anatole would leave my father. And no one on this plantation would watch you, my wife, locked away without lifting a hand. You don't know what you are saying. Come, let Rachel put you to bed."

"No! I don't want her."

"Claire—"

"I won't have her, do you hear me? And you can't just leave. You have to do something about Belle-Marie. You have to! She is in the swamp with the panther. He will—"

"Very well. Don't upset yourself again." Justin's voice was stern. "Come," he said again with a softer inflection. "No more hysterics. Get into bed."

"No," she said, tugging to free herself from his grip. "Go away and leave me alone. All of you."

Then as Justin's hold began to tighten and a dangerous look came into his eyes, she felt Octavia move to her side.

"Let me, Justin," the older woman said, deftly separating Claire from his hands.

Over her shoulder she spoke to Rachel. "I won't need you. You may go."

Claire was relieved when Justin stepped back, relieved to be free of his anger. But she knew that a look passed between Octavia and her husband over her head, and she was troubled.

When the others had gone, Octavia moved silently to undress her and bathe her hands and face as if she were a child. There was comfort in her silence and her soft, sure movements. And even though she could not quite trust her, Claire found herself asking, as Octavia returned from the other room carrying a decanter in one hand and a glass in the other, "You do believe me, don't you?"

The older woman carefully poured a measure of brandy into the glass and then handed it to her. "You are a sensible girl, not prone to fits of nerves, a good trait for—for any woman. In most cases I would be inclined to listen to you."

Claire hardly realized that Octavia had avoided a direct answer. "Justin didn't believe me. But it did happen, Octavia, it did. There was a note. What did I do—I must have dropped it on the washstand. That will prove—oh, but Justin must have seen that. It was addressed to him—" She trailed off, refusing to consider the implications of the line of thought.

"I see no note," Octavia said after a glance around. "But don't upset yourself. Drink this, it will help you to sleep." She closed Claire's nerveless fingers around the cool sides of the glass.

As if taking medicine, Claire swallowed the contents, coughing a little. Then staring up at Octavia, she handed the glass back to her. What if it contained poison, she wondered. She had not thought soon enough.

Octavia did not speak, and in that silence Claire suddenly became aware of a woman weeping. It came from far away, and for a second she was not sure whether the sound was real or only in her mind. Without speaking, she met Octavia's eyes.

Octavia nodded. "It is Helene that you hear. We were all searching for her this evening. She disappeared just before sundown. You wouldn't know, of course—we didn't want to disturb you. Rachel—your maid—said you were resting in your room and did not want to be disturbed. We found Helene and brought her home, just now, when we found you here. Berthe is attending to her."

"She isn't hurt?" Claire asked, the blood-stained face of Belle-Marie before her again.

"No, I don't think so. We found her in the woods where Gerard was killed. She was just sitting there, crying. I don't know what's gotten into her lately. She is just as she was after Gerard's death." For a moment her eyes rested broodingly on Claire's face. "I don't know what's gotten into everyone."

For a long while, Claire lay on her bed tossing restlessly, until perspiration dampened her hair and made her nightgown cling to her. Her thoughts spun in circles, an endless wheel of questions without answers. Justin did not come, and from the sounds that penetrated from the other rooms of the house, few of the others sought their beds. Footsteps and hushed voices disturbed her. More than once she sat up, trying to hear, wondering what was happening.

Her head began to ache and her eyes to feel sore from straining to see in the darkness around her. The mosquito *baire* seemed to shut the air out, and in an abrupt exasperation, she thrust her pillows and bolster onto the floor. Then as she lay back, there was a swimming sensation in her head, and a grayness like fainting engulfed her.

She came awake suddenly, every nerve stretched with an aching awareness. She felt chilled. Dazedly, she raised a hand to her face. The skin was dry and burning to the touch. She got out of bed and padded across the room in her bare feet, moving with an unerring instinct through the midnight dark. She did not even glance at Justin's bed. She seemed to know that he was not in it. At the door she paused, then shaking off caution, she turned the knob and passed through the door.

There was the sound of breathing coming from Octavia's bed. She stared for a moment at the still form beneath the sheet, then moved on, slipping into the dining room. It was black in this room, but she hardly slowed her pace. She reached out to touch the back of a chair at the table, then using the others as a guide, running her hand over their carved backs, she made her way to the double doors, skirting the sideboard where silver chimed as she brushed against it.

The salon, as she entered, was not quite as dark as the dining room, but still she kicked against a stool. The noise sent alarm fluttering along her veins, but her ankle did not hurt her.

It was not hard to find Berthe's door. She simply slid her fingers along the wall until she touched the frame. The knob turned easily beneath her fingers, and the panel swung inward, as if on oiled hinges.

She paused on the threshold. In this room the curtains were still open, as if they had never been pulled for the night. The bed was a flat surface in the darkness, the bedside table a dim outline beside it. Where was Berthe? Still with Helene? But those were questions of little meaning. Her quest was more important, much more important.

A draught fanned the hair that hung about her

shoulders, and she shivered in sudden cold as it moved over her heated skin. She swayed slightly as she stood there, but was unaware of either sensation.

She moved in a trance toward the table, her hands outstretched, reaching. She touched cold metal.

"Ah," she said, a fierce satisfaction in the sound. "The death mask."

With an abnormally heightened sense of touch, she traced the features of the mask. It was as she remembered it, she thought, her fingers curling around the edges.

All at once she could see the glow of the bronze in her hands. Light grew in the room.

Then a scream rent the air!

The death mask fell from Claire's hands, striking the floor with a metallic clang, to lie face up at her feet. She swung around to see Berthe, a lamp in her hands, standing in the doorway. The woman stepped back a pace, one hand going to her heart.

"What are you doing in my room?" she said, her lips white with fear, though with a strange clarity Claire knew that the fear was for the safety of her possessions.

As Claire stood mute, the other woman took a tentative step into the room. "Did you want something? I have just this moment come from Helene. She is not herself, poor thing. Not that I mind sitting with her, even though she doesn't appreciate it. I don't usually sleep much." There was a suspicious gleam in her small eyes as they darted from the mask on the floor to Claire's gown and her hair loose about her bare arms and shoulders.

Claire returned her gaze with the wide eyes of one who has been awakened too quickly. She was trembling from head to foot, but she seemed unaware of it. She could hear hurrying footsteps.

Berthe moved closer, her voice insistent. "What was it, Claire. Tell me what you wanted."

"It was the death mask—" Claire could recognize the whisper as her own, and yet she felt remote from the sound. "There was—something—about the mask. I don't know—"

Frowning, she lowered her gaze slowly to the mask that lay at her feet. "I can't think. There was something. I almost knew—before you came. Marcel. He knows. He tried to—tell me."

"Tried to tell you what?"

The question broke into her train of thought, and she returned to the beginning in an attempt to understand herself, more than to explain her actions to Berthe.

"I thought—I thought if I saw it again. I almost knew. I think I—almost remembered. Marcel. I must ask Marcel. He can tell me."

Then Octavia was there, drawn by Berthe's scream, and beyond in the doorway was Justin, still wearing the clothes he had worn earlier, the toes of his boots wet with dew. He began to move, wavering in her distorted view. She felt herself wafted up, floating hazily.

"What was that she was saying, about Marcel?"

"Who knows? Delirious, poor child, and burning up with fever. We must get her back to bed or she will be really ill."

An almost unbearable warmth enveloped her. For a moment panic beat against her throat. Then, like smoke, she drifted away.

"What!"

A simple word, and yet the tone of horror in which it was spoken pierced the mists of Claire's drug-induced sleep.

"Dead, both of them."

That voice, she knew it. But not Justin. Oh. Edouard.

"How can it be?" Octavia spoke from near her bed, her voice thick with incipient tears. Claire wanted to open her eyes, to look about her, but they seemed to be weighted. She lay still, listening, but though she understood what they were saying, the meaning seemed to lack reality for her.

"The outside door was open. Anatole had a knife in his back. And the head of a rooster was lying on the floor beside him."

"And—and Marcel?"

"A stroke, at least that is what it looks like. One has to wonder if it could be that Marcel saw who killed Anatole and it was too much for his heart."

"Oh, Edouard, what a terrible thing to think."

"There are worse things. It could be—"

"No, no. Don't tell me. I don't want to know."

It was part of the nightmare. It must be. They could not really be dead, not Marcel with his gentle eyes, and the silent but alert Anatole. Who would kill Marcel's servant, and why? Even as the question formed in her mind she heard Octavia echo it.

"Who would do such a thing?"

"Who knows?" Edouard answered, his voice ragged. "But it has the appearance of a servants' quarrel. You know how quickly these things blow up. There were quite a few who envied Anatole his position in the big house with the old master. He had probably made his share of enemies. He was always a bit above himself, in my opinion."

Yes. Anatole had enemies, Claire remembered. He had defied the voodoo to come to her aid in the jail. Now he was dead, with a voodoo symbol by his side. And because of his death, Justin's father had died. They were both dead because of her. It was too much, too much to bear. The blackness smothered the bitter thoughts in her mind like snuffing a candle.

She slept, and the hours slid by one after another, filled with dreams and confusion, daylight and dark. Sometimes a voice babbled in her head of blood and death and knives and cats with burning eyes, of dying cockerels and of blood again. Sometimes the taste of medicine lingered on her tongue. And in the times of her greatest confusion, a voice came and whispered in her ear that those who died would have lived if it had not been for her. That she herself had killed them. That life was a burden not worth the lifting, and death a friend who took away pain.

Then once, when the nightmare was closing in around her, the beat of its cold wings was banished by a sensation of closeness and comfort.

She opened her eyes. Her cheek lay against fine white lawn and strong arms encircled her.

"*Pauvre petite,*" a low voice murmured against

her hair. "What have I done to you? I never intended it. I saw your golden loveliness, your soft nature and sympathetic heart, and I had to have you. You are the one really lovely thing that ever came into my life. I planned so much for us. But our marriage, like everything else I touch, has withered in my hands." His voice had the timbre of someone saying goodbye to a dream. Could it be the voice of a murderer, a cold-blooded mutilator of women, or even a parricide? It did not seem so.

But perhaps she preferred to delude herself? She preferred not to believe that the man whose heart beat so strongly beneath her temple could kill his former mistress simply because she dared to blackmail him and to touch that which belonged to him, his legal wife. She preferred to ignore that streak of righteous anger that had caused him to kill his uncle so many years before. But what possible reason could he have for killing Anatole? Or did it follow necessarily that the same person was guilty of both crimes? Might it not be as it seemed, that Belle-Marie's death was the revenge of the Voodooienne for flaunting her authority?

She did not know. Still, when Justin had pressed his lips to hers with a tender desperation, lain her gently against her pillows and gone away, her mind was clear.

If it was not Justin, if he was not the murderer, then who?

Tentatively she approached the question, fearful that she would be thrust back into the nightmare of dread that she had just left. A dread that was filled with fear only because it involved the man who had just left her; the dread that there was no one else who could possibly be guilty.

Who else? There must be someone. Ben perhaps? The overseer had been drawn to the quadroon. If she had spurned him he might have taken her life. Or Octavia? But why? Octavia was loyal to Justin and took an intense interest in his affairs, but would she murder to protect him? Helene? She had threatened to have Belle-Marie whipped and she had been wandering the grounds in an emotional state the night the quadroon died, but would she have committed murder? Could she have killed as an act of revenge delayed ten long years? Could Helene, acting with the diabolical cruelty of some mythological goddess, have killed the loved one of her son because her son had killed her own lover? Oh, surely not. Berthe then, but that quiet, pallid woman, intent on her husband's memory would have been no match for the bold and primitive Belle-Marie. On top of that she had no reason. Her son, Edouard? The same thing applied to him, no reason. In fact, no one in this house had anything to gain by the three deaths.

Something at the back of her mind tried to struggle forward, but though she stared at the wall before her as it turned crimson with the light of the setting sun, she could not draw the memory from the recesses of her own consciousness.

So absorbed was she in her thoughts that she hardly noticed when the color drained from the sky and the gray shadows of evening crept into the room.

For a time, Octavia's great black cat lay across

her knees, purring. She could not remember the last time she had noticed him, and she smoothed his fur, glad of his company at that moment, his quiet companionship a welcome accompaniment to the day's end. But when the drifting smells of supper being cooked drew him toward the kitchen, she did not try to keep him.

Chapter Eleven

It may have been a half an hour later when Berthe slipped into the room carrying a small glass on a hand tray.

"Ah, you are better," she said, her eyes moving over Claire's face, noting the clearness of her eyes. "No one told me."

Claire smiled at the surprise on the woman's voice. "I'm not sure anyone knows," she replied in a voice that she was startled to find much weaker than her usual tones. "I seem to have just gotten rid of my muddled head, and I don't believe that I have fever now at all."

"That is good," Berthe said, nodding with a thoughtful expression in her eyes.

"I have been lying here wondering where Octavia is. This seems to be the first time I have awakened that she was not near."

"Very true. She has stayed by you night and day. Now she is indulging in a much-needed rest. I confess I helped her. I put a bit of laudanum in her cordial, and suggested that she lie down. She was exhausted, quite done-in, and I'm sure she will thank me for it."

A spasm of disquiet seized Claire, then was gone as quickly as it had come. "What has become of Justin? He was here a little while ago, and it can't be too long until time to dress for supper?"

"I saw him walking toward the cemetery, my dear, to visit his father's grave. You know how close Justin was to his father. We had some rain yesterday. There will be repair work to be done, a new grave, you know? Helene is in her room sleeping, too, though there was no need for me to give her a sedative. She has shown me the door. She insists that I drive her to distraction and give her the migraine. But at least she is certain to remain behind her door. My son has gone to the neighbors. I, myself, gave him the message. It will be some little time before he returns, but I hope we need not wait supper on him. So you see? All is quiet. We are alone, and it is time to tidy up the last details."

She held out the tray as she spoke, and before her last words had registered, Claire had taken the small glass into her hand.

"Details?"

"Don't trouble yourself, Claire, dear. Just drink your medicine, there's a good girl."

"I don't feel ill anymore. I don't want it." It smelled strongly of laudanum mixed with wine, medicine she remembered taking several times these last few days, but she could not bring herself to drink it.

"Never mind what you want. It is good for you."

Berthe's cryptic statements, the intent look of her eyes, her unusually purposeful manner, sent a shiver of alarm along Claire's veins. She remembered the other times that poison had been served to her in her room. When she raised the glass to her lips, she barely touched them with the liquid.

"Drink it down now," Berthe insisted.

Claire made a face and her gaze rested on the vase on the table beside the bed, a vase containing a large, spreading bouquet of honeysuckle and wild roses.

"Nothing that is good for you ever tastes good. You must drink it."

Once more Claire raised the glass to her lips, then she went still, her head tilted, a listening expression on her still features.

"What is it?" Berthe exclaimed. "Is it Justin?" She hastened to the french door and pulled aside the curtains.

Her ruse had worked. Quickly, noiselessly, Claire tipped the glass into the vase. It filled to the brim, leaving a small amount of liquid in the glass. As Berthe turned back she hastily put the glass once more to her mouth then brought it down with a shudder.

"That is all I can stand," she told the other woman, holding out the glass with closed eyes. It could be that she was behaving in a ridiculous panic. Surely now that Belle-Marie was dead there was no longer anyone who would have reason to harm her? But someone had killed Belle-Marie. And since she really did not want the cordial, she was glad that it reposed in the vase. It would do no harm to the porcelain, and Berthe's feelings would not be hurt by her refusal to take the medicine from her hand.

Berthe stared at the glass, then made a faint movement with her shoulder before accepting it with a part of her attention still on the window.

"Was it not Justin? I could have sworn—"

"I didn't see him. You must have been imagining things again. Just lie back now, Claire, and wait. You haven't been at all well. In truth I am amazed to see you so bright."

Claire thought of Justin and the way he held her in his arms, and she smiled.

"In fact," Berthe went on, taking a seat in the slipper chair that had been pulled up beside the bed, "you seem to be quite your old self, but still you cannot get too much rest. I will just sit here with you until you drop off."

She wished the woman would go and leave her in peace. The fact that she intended to stay a while troubled her, though she could not have said why. "You needn't sit with me if you have other things to do," she said, hiding her uneasiness. "It isn't as if I were truly ill."

"Oh, no. But you must allow me to do this. I have nothing more to do."

Claire subsided, and quiet descended over the room. Darkness was growing outside, filling the room with dim shadows. It was time for the lamps to be lit, but Berthe made no move to do so. For herself, she did not mind. There was nothing she wanted to see. She thought of Octavia and Helene and Edouard and Justin and also of Berthe who sat beside her bed and the way their lives had become entangled in these past few weeks. It was inevitable that they should, and yet there was something fascinating about the way the course of lives could be changed by a trivial incident. If Edouard had never used the knife on Justin's face she would not be lying here, and, in all probability, Gerard Leroux would not have died. Marcel would not have been paralyzed, Helene would not be the lonely and embittered woman she was. It was frightening, and yet, comforting, to realize that nothing in life depended only on herself. She could not control her destiny alone, but then neither did she have to bear the whole responsibility for the course it took.

"Claire?"

Her concentration was so great that it was a moment before she answered. "Yes?"

"I thought perhaps you had fallen asleep."

"No," she said hesitantly, her voice soft.

"Well, I'm sure you will," Berthe said, getting to her feet. She moved across the room in the dark, and Claire thought she was leaving. Then she heard the grate of the key in the lock.

"Berthe?"

She heard the rustle of the woman's clothing as she turned and moved back toward the bed.

"Poor Claire. It is hard. But you see, you should never have married Justin."

"What do you mean?" Claire asked, ignoring the trace of sadness in the woman's voice. She had nearly, in that quiet interval, persuaded herself that her alarm was for nothing, but now it returned in full force, and she closed her hands tightly on the covers to keep herself from crying out.

"Why shouldn't I tell you? You won't live to repeat it. Already the overdose of laudanum I have given you is deadening your senses. Soon you will rest in the sleep that knows no awakening—but just listen to me. I grow poetic. How droll."

That quiet voice. How well it leant itself to irony.

"Berthe—"

"Soon now Justin will return. When he walks through the door I will throw this knife I have in my sleeve and it will bury itself in his heart. When I arrange the body, it will appear that he plunged it into his own breast after administering the drugged wine to you. A tragic tableau, don't you think? But Justin's past and his personality lends itself so well to such a gesture."

"No one will believe it," Claire whispered, then added, "least of all Octavia."

"I grant you she will find it hard. But it is easy to further blacken the character of one who is already black enough. Added to that, you and he have shown such signs of distress lately. Besides, murder with suicide has happened time and again in history, why not once more? Then, what else is there for them to think? That it was I? Can you conceive of anything more unlikely? All these years of being meek and pitiable, accepting charity and harsh words alike. But it will be worth it when my son inherits Sans Songe. The meek, you will remember, inherit the earth."

"You will never be able—to kill—Justin."

"You think not? It takes no great strength to throw a knife the way my own Gerard taught me so many years ago. It takes only nerve and a certain dexterity of the wrist. When Justin enters this room from that outside door he will present a perfect target. He will never know what struck him."

"You can't do this."

"I would not have had to, were it not for you," she said, reasonably, as she moved to the washstand. "So you see it really is all your fault, a fact I have been trying to impress upon you these last few days when I could see you alone." She took a tinderbox from her pocket and proceeded to light a single candle. The room slowly came to life with the dim illumination, and Claire stared at Berthe, trying to see if there was any difference in the woman's colorless face and figure. There was little that she could see, except for a glitter in her small eyes and the sureness of the smile that was set on her pale lips.

"Justin," she mused, "so very obliging of him to take the blame for his uncle's death. I never expected that, or that he would set out to destroy himself with drink, duels, and dissipation when society turned against him. He was doing a masterly job of it, and I quite thought he would succeed until he married you."

"And now you want us both dead."

"But, of course, for Edouard, my son. Is that so hard to understand? He and I have lived off the charity of this family too long. My husband helped make this plantation. He worked just as hard as Marcel. But Marcel was the elder, the one with the money and influence, the one who received the grant of land from the Crown when they arrived from France. And so my Gerard got nothing. It wasn't fair. It wasn't fair for Justin, who is not even a legitimate heir, to have everything while my son has nothing!" Her voice had risen, until she was almost shouting.

"What?" Claire asked, unable to make sense of the last diatribe.

"Are you so shocked? Don't you know Justin was not Marcel's son? He is Octavia's by-blow. It was for her and her child's sake that Marcel brought Helene, that common woman, fifteen years his junior, into this house. He brought her here to put a good light on Octavia's shame and to provide himself with an heir just to keep my Gerard from inheriting as he should have!"

"I think," Justin said, his voice quiet, but carrying a definite note of menace, "that you had better explain."

In their preoccupation, they had failed to hear Justin approaching. Now he stood in the doorway.

Berthe made a quick movement to bring the knife from her sleeve into her hand. It gleamed as it slid into view, but though Claire uttered a cry of warning, the woman did not throw it. She seemed more intent on the damage she could do with her tongue. Still, she was wary. As if to keep him in perspective, she fell back a step.

"Don't order me, Justin. I have no qualms about killing you. You stand in the way of my son, but you are also to blame for what I have become. Your father, your real father, died leaving Octavia alone and unwed. Marcel took Helene to wife. She was of good family but poor, and so Marcel, a well-to-do bachelor, was a matrimonial prize, even if he was nearly old enough to be her father. Helene agreed to pretend to be your mother—the prospect of a trip abroad was the bait, I believe. They lived for a time in England, but the weather was bad for Marcel's health, so they went to Portugal. They would have preferred France, but it was too unsettled there. The three of them lived in seclusion in a small town on the coast until you were born, then they returned with you in Helene's arms.

"But Helene soon grew bored with motherhood. She began to look around her for amusement, and so she began a flirtation that lasted nearly twenty years, right under Marcel's nose. What did you think, Justin? That it would be better for everyone to think that you had killed your uncle rather than for your father to bear the mark of Cain? Did you really think Marcel had killed his brother in a jealous rage?"

Claire stared at Justin. Not a muscle moved in his face. There was nothing to tell her whether it was he or his father who had killed his uncle.

"And so—I married," he said gently.

"You married, and there was Claire, a beautiful, healthy bride, who would be sure to present you with an heir before the year was out, destroying my Edouard's chances of succession forever. I knew of Belle-Marie and I knew of her connection with the voodoo priestess. The priestess was her mother."

"It was you," Claire said in horror, staring at the knife in Berthe's hand, and thinking of the torn and bleeding face. "It was you who killed her."

"Yes. It was not hard. Belle-Marie felt only contempt for me, too, and that was—fatal. I couldn't stay to do away with you then, though I wanted to. The panther was about, hunting. I hoped he would find you and kill you for me."

"Why did you kill Belle-Marie? What reason could you have?"

"She was so stupid," Berthe said, her mouth

twisted with scorn. "I sent a message to her in New Orleans as soon as I heard of the nuptials. I told her to come here and together we would rid ourselves of you, Claire. With a little judicious black magic, a threat to the coachman who died, poor man, we arranged for the coach to go off the bridge. Then that fool Belle-Marie tried to poison you without consulting me. I suppose she thought I might object to poison in the house, or perhaps it was the voodoo. She could be secretive about that at times. She believed in it. Not I! And her charms, her *gris-gris*, her power, where were they to help her when the time came? But because of the poison, I was fooled for a time into thinking that Claire was *enciente*. I had to hurry, and so the bungled attempt the night of the voodoo ceremony."

Claire could feel Justin's gaze on her face, but she would not look at him. She had not told him of that night.

"Then the silly fool, besotted with you, Justin, caught on that it was not only Claire that I wanted dead. I could not depend on you not to remarry. You had married once, you might do it again.

"But you wanted to know why I killed Belle-Marie. I was waiting in the swamp for you when she came. We quarreled and she said she would come to you and warn you, tell you what I was doing. I could not let her do that. She was not hard to kill. I waited until she began to walk away, and then I threw my knife. Then I savaged her with it, to make it look as if Claire had done it, a crime of jealousy, you know. I waited for you, Justin, but you didn't come. I was going to kill you near Belle-Marie. It would look as if Claire had caught you together, then if the law did not take care of Claire, I rather guessed that it would not be hard to have her die later, an apparent suicide."

"Justin," Claire cried, as she saw him start toward Berthe. He stopped, but he did not take his eyes from Berthe's face.

"No, don't try it. I can't miss at this distance. Gerard would be proud of me."

"Proud!" Claire turned to her in disgust.

"Oh, yes. 'Living is a game of wit,' he always said, and he congratulated anyone, even himself, who played it well. Such as the game he played with Helene for so many years."

Gerard. The man of the death mask.

"It was you," she said without thinking. "The game Gerard played with Helene hurt you as well as Marcel. And you killed Gerard for it. You killed your husband."

She saw Justin grow suddenly still, but she could not give him her full attention.

When Berthe's voice came it was a whisper. "I did. I carried the case of dueling pistols with me, and when Helene left him, there in the woods where they had met, I loaded one of the pistols and I shot him as he came walking toward me. I didn't hear Marcel coming. When he saw what had happened, he began to run, and then he clutched his chest and fell down, so it didn't matter that he had seen. I thought he was dead, too; he might as well have been from the way he looked. So I put the pistol I had fired in his hand, and I loaded the other one and put it at Gerard's side. Then I left the box lying there in the grass and walked away. How was I to know that Marcel was not dead? How was I to guess that Justin would be close enough to hear the shot, or that he would come upon them and rearrange it all so as to take the blame upon himself?"

"You let him think all these years that the man he considered his father had killed his own brother."

"Why not? Marcel could not deny it. As soon as I found that out, I was safe, at least I thought I was until you said that Marcel could tell you about the mask. But after it was over, I was glad. Gerard would never be able to leave me. All those years, and Gerard had said it was a game. But then I heard them say they were going away together, Helene and my husband. Their children, they said, were grown. They no longer owed anyone anything. But they were only middle-aged lovers trying to breathe life into their tired love affair. So exciting, to run away together. It was disgusting. Gerard actually said he had nothing to hold him. Nothing! But he was my husband! Mine!"

"And you kept him."

"I kept him!"

Possessiveness shrilled in her voice, the same possessiveness, Claire thought, that made her cling to Gerard's belongings, his clothes, his jewelry, canes and wigs, and his centuries-old knives.

Suddenly, from the corner of her eye, Claire saw Justin's fingers clenching into a fist. He was going to try to disarm Berthe. She could feel it. She must distract the woman somehow.

"But did you keep him?" she asked, raising her voice. "You don't mourn him. You never loved him, only what he could give you. Helene is the one who has kept his memory alive in her heart, despite all your show of the things that were his. In the end it is Helene who has kept him!"

Rage burned in Berthe's narrow eyes. "You—why isn't the laudanum working? I gave you enough— but I don't need laudanum to silence you." She leaned toward Claire, vindictiveness in her twisted face. The knife rose glinting in the candlelight. Claire threw up her arm to protect her head, and then the blade began to fall.

At that instant, Justin reached her, spun her around, reaching for her wrist. But the knife continued its descent as he missed his grip, and slashed through his clothes. Claire saw with terror the spasm of pain that crossed his face, then the knife clattered to the floor and Berthe sagged, the wild, reckless courage of evil draining from her as she felt Justin's greater strength.

Justin flung her into a chair, picked the knife up from where it had fallen, and reached out to draw Claire into the circle of his arm. "Claire, *ma coeur*," he said huskily. "What is this that she gave you? Was it poison?"

"It is nothing. I didn't take it," she answered, the words rushing off her tongue. "But you, I saw her strike you—"

In a sudden flurry of skirts, Berthe, so slack a moment before, jumped to her feet and ran, leaving the french door open behind her.

"Justin!" Claire cried, but he shook his head.

"Let her go. There is no place she can run."

They listened to her footfalls fading along the gallery. There was silence. Then a terrible scream split the night!

Before its last echoes had died, they were stand

ing at the gallery railing. Nothing moved in the dark, there was no noise to show there was any living thing near. Then beneath them, a figure seemed to materialize from out of the darkness.

Claire recognized the Voodooienne the second before she began to speak. Her voice was soft and rich with sadness.

"Monsieur Justin, if you are worried about that one, that Madame Berthe, you need not worry anymore. I learned, me, that she killed my Belle-Marie in the swamp. I know, too, that she has killed the Monsieur Marcel's man, Anatole, and then put the pillow over the Still One's face until he, too, is dead so that she and her son can have all in peace without fear."

"How do you know these things?"

"I am told."

It was the only answer she was going to give. Justin did not press her.

"Berthe—we heard a scream," Claire said, unable to resist the question. "What happened to her?"

"Ah, madame," the woman said in a voice that could hardly be heard where they stood. "Ah, madame, it is best not to ask."

Chapter Twelve

A KNOCK SOUNDED on the bedroom door. Rachel, very subdued, but with the lines of tension gone from her face, moved to answer it. When Claire saw Octavia standing there, she smiled at the maid. "That will be all. I won't need you until morning."

"Yes, madame," the girl murmured, and flashing a shy smile, stepped outside and closed the door behind Octavia.

The older woman was not the same either. She stood clasping and unclasping her hands. She still wore her Arabic robe, but it no longer seemed bizarre. Her eyes were shadowed and her lips were pale and trembling.

Justin spoke from the bed where he lay propped on pillows in the great four-poster bed, a bandage white against his olive skin, spanning his chest. "Come in, Aunt Octavia. I haven't thanked you properly for seeing to the slash on my side."

She gave him a quick, hesitant smile, and glanced toward Claire before she looked back to her son.

"You look very well, considering. But you must not be surprised if you feel feverish tomorrow."

"No, I won't. But don't stand there. Come and sit down."

"Yes, let me get you a chair," Claire said, dragging one of the slipper chairs forward. Octavia sat down, but she scarcely seemed to realize what she was doing.

"Justin, I—they are saying in the quarters—again after all these years—that Berthe said—Berthe told that—I—I am your mother."

Justin was quiet for a moment. "Yes, she said that. Aren't you?"

Claire looked away. She felt that she ought not to be here, witnessing this. It was too private. These two people, each wary of the other, each afraid of being hurt, were yet tied by the strongest of bonds. Justin had given Octavia a way out. She had only to deny him, to claim what Berthe had said was the hysterical ravings of a madwoman. She did not do that.

"Yes, I am your mother." Her fingers were clasped in her lap, she sat straight, and suddenly proud, on the edge of her chair.

Justin sighed. "I'm glad," he said, smiling.

Tears rose in Octavia's eyes. "You—you look like the Lerouxs, you know, not at all like your father. I think I have regretted that at times. He was a good man, your father, of good family, a French nobleman, handsome, kind, and—you must believe me—honorable."

"Yes, thank you—maman—for that."

"It was not easy, giving you into Helene's care. She loved you well enough, as a child, when she gradually grew used to the idea that she and Marcel would never have children of their own. But older children distress some women, make them feel their age, and they grow nervous and irritable with them. I have been afraid that you would hate me, but it seemed the best, to let you be Marcel's son rather than my—mistake. I was always there. I would not marry, even when I could. I would not go away to another man's house and leave you." Her voice broke and she could not go on.

"Please," Claire said, putting a hand on her shoulder. "I'm sure there is no need to explain. Justin understands, and I also. Don't do this to yourself."

"I—I must. It is the price—" She stopped speaking, and fumbling with her wide sleeve, wiped her eyes and swallowed. "Marcel must have known he could never have children. We did not speak of it, but he registered your birth in Portugal under his own name with that of Helene as the mother. It was not hard. It was a small village and we were unknown. For all time you are legally his son. Only Helene could question it, and she does not dare, not so long as she is dependent on you for her comfort. So you see, nothing is changed."

"Yes, I see. If that is what you want. It will be, always, as you say, *maman*. Come, don't sit there across the room as though you were afraid of me. I am not so childishly moral that the matter of a few marriage lines are so great a tragedy. Smile and dry your tears and—" But Octavia had cast herself upon him, crying all the harder. Then she jumped up.

"Your wound!" she cried and kissed him, laughing through her tears as she stood back.

"You know it is little more than a scratch."

"No such thing. You must be careful, or it will start to bleed again."

"Yes, *maman*," he agreed in a voice of exaggerated docility.

"And do not use those words in that tone or I will—I will box your ears!" she said, but her laugh was shaky. She grew grave, then took a deep breath.

"Perhaps it would be best if—if you did not use the words at all. It is not such an important thing, to be called *maman*. Many people request their children to call them by their first names, and I have grown used to 'Aunt Octavia' on your lips. After all these years, shall we change? When so many of our friends and relatives are most definitely too moral to understand? If not for your sake and mine, then for your children and my grandchildren?"

"Have I not said it will be as you wish? Do not distress yourself, my dear aunt."

She smiled at him tremulously, and he reached out and caught her hand, pressing it, before he changed the subject.

"So, Edouard has gone, at this time of the night?"

"About an hour ago. He did not look well. This has been a great shock to him. He had begun to suspect something, since Berthe was often gone from her room, walking. And once before he missed the knife from his collection that Berthe used to kill Belle-Marie. It was generous of you to offer to let him stay, but I think he will be much better, more his own man, somewhere else, especially with the stake you gave him."

Had Edouard been so innocent of Berthe's plotting for his sake, Claire wondered. She hoped so, but she was not sorry to see him go. If he had stayed, they would never have been able to forget. And also, though it pained her to admit it, beneath the veneer of politeness she had felt obligated to show him, she had never been able to forgive him for his mutilation of Justin's face.

"I see you have not dismissed Rachel," Octavia was saying.

"No, she never wanted to harm me. She was afraid, not of what Belle-Marie would do to her so much as what she might do to her family in the quarters. She was terrified the whole time. You remember that the coachman who died drove my carriage. Rachel knew he had been told to upset my carriage and make it look like an accident. She had been told to carry the poisoned food to my room and then to decoy me to the jail so that Justin could be lured to the swamp."

"Only he never saw the note. It must have fallen to the floor where you found it."

"Yes. But the point is, Rachel was frightened of being found out at the big house, but she was more frightened of failing at her assigned tasks. She said that everyone in the quarters thinks the coachman died because he failed, and so she lived in constant fear. I, too, have lived in fear. I know what she felt, and so I think she has suffered enough. Beside, the Voodooienne, Belle-Marie's mother, is still very much alive. Rachel is afraid to go back to the quarters for fear of her."

Octavia shook her head. "This voodoo. Will it ever die out?"

"Not so long as ignorance lives," Justin answered her.

And as if the subject reminded her, Octavia said, "Ben has gone. He had, from what the grapevine says, developed a *tendre* for Belle-Marie. It also says that her mother was not pleased. Whether her death has upset him, or the priestess has threatened him with worms in his ears, snakes in his stomach, or one of her more inelegant curses, he is no longer with us."

"Our circle grows slimmer. You, Claire and I, and Helene. How will we manage?" Justin asked wearily.

"You mean how will we face each other over the dinner table?" Octavia smiled. "We will do well, we three. As for Helene, I think she will be better for the change. Half her brooding and her moods could be laid at Berthe's door. She was good at subtle, poisonous reminders. Berthe knew that Helene blamed herself for turning Justin, so she thought, into a murderer. But instead of being contrite, it was Helene's way to hide her guilt with defiance. Perhaps she, too, can have peace now, and can forget."

"I was thinking of Marcel—"

"Don't. It does no good, my son, to dwell on the things that cause us to suffer in the remembrance. Marcel hated his existence these ten years. Now he is free. Let him go."

"Perhaps you are right," Justin said, but looked away, his jaw tightening.

There was a moment of quiet. To Claire, Justin looked tired. Glancing at Octavia, she saw her smile as their eyes met in understanding, and she got to her feet.

The door had hardly closed behind her before Justin turned to her. "Now a few answers, if you please. Why didn't you tell me?"

She did not pretend to misunderstand him. "I did, or at least, I tried to. I told you of the jail and of the *gris-gris* in New Orleans and here. But you acted as though you didn't believe me. You looked at me as if you thought I was imagining things."

"It was difficult to believe of Belle-Marie. I had grown used to—"

He stopped, and Claire, half in anger, finished for him. "—to a complaisant mistress bowing to your every wish."

He did not answer, and color sprang to her cheekbones. She looked away, aware that jealousy rang in the remark. To cover it, she went on.

"I didn't tell you of the poison, because I was never certain, never had proof. You knew I had been ill, however. It was the cause of those rumors."

"Morning sickness." He grinned with a lazy wickedness.

"It wasn't funny to me."

"Not then."

"No, and now that you bring it up I don't believe you were amused either, at the time."

The grin vanished. "I heard nothing from you about this voodoo ceremony," he accused.

"No, I—went with Octavia. The cat, Bast, was sick. Octavia seemed to think that the Voodooienne could cure him—and she did, Justin. He was poisoned, I'm sure. He had eaten my dinner."

He shrugged. "If she knew the poison, perhaps she knew the antidote. For all their spells and bits of bones, there is some practical medicine, more than most people realize or care to acknowledge, in their art."

"The ceremony was horrible."

"I can imagine."

She was not sure that he could imagine the savagery of Belle-Marie in that voodoo dance. She found it hard to believe that he could know of that side of his former mistress and still have kept her, but perhaps Belle-Marie had only become so wild after being turned out of his keeping.

"I ran away from the dancing and the drums, and someone followed me. Berthe, of course, but I thought at first it was one of the men. They were—excited. And then the knife was thrown."

"And you came home and smiled and never mentioned the matter—to anyone."

"I—thought after the attempt on my life that it had been Belle-Marie. She was there, dancing. I thought perhaps she had meant to kill me there, near the crowd, where the crime could be blamed on drunkenness and frenzy, and no one would be able to say who had done it. I brought the knife home with me, but I didn't think you would believe me. And I suppose somewhere in my mind I was suspicious of Octavia, because she had persuaded me to go with her, you see, and then left me alone.

Then I lost the knife, so I had no proof, and I didn't know whom to trust."

"Because the knife belonged to Edouard? If only you had told me—But no, I don't know if I could have connected the knife to Berthe. All these years, and I never guessed. It seems impossible." He paused a moment, staring into space before he went on.

"But you were wrong, I would have believed you. I did from the beginning, but I didn't want to alarm you by appearing to be overly worried by it. I questioned Sylvest, the groom who rode beside the coachman. He told me that he thought the man might have deliberately backed the coach off the bridge, but the coachman was dead. He could neither defend himself nor tell me anything of who had asked him to do such a thing."

"What of the man I saw," Claire asked suddenly, "a man wearing a caped greatcoat like yours?"

"What man?"

"Sitting his horse, watching the coach go off the bridge, watching me in the water."

Justin shook his head. "Many men wear greatcoats. It could have been any passing stranger, or might it not have been a woman, Berthe, wearing a coat, perhaps one of Edouard's, against the rain, coming to view her handiwork?"

"It might have been," Claire agreed slowly, thinking of that figure on the horse, so indistinct in the rain and early morning gloom.

"Claire?"

She looked up at him, caught by a sternness in his voice.

"It was not I."

"I know," she said, and suddenly she did and was able to smile, to return his gaze without letting her own waver.

When he saw that she was telling the truth, his black eyes grew less shadowed and a hint of a smile curved his mouth before he continued. "Belle-Marie was not here at the time of the accident with the coach, so there seemed little reason to connect her with it. Because of that, I did not go and demand an answer, even when you told me of the *gris-gris*. Such a visit could be so easily misunderstood in an isolated society like the plantation where every move is watched. I did believe you were in danger, but the evidence was so insubstantial that there seemed no way to protect you, other than confining you to the house, and even that was no guarantee, was it? The last thing I wanted to do, however, was to upset you and have you demand to be taken back to New Orleans. I was afraid if I ever allowed you to leave me, you would never come back."

Leaving that interesting declaration for the moment, Claire said, "But if you were not with Belle-Marie, where were you when you left me during the day—and sometimes at night?"

"Working. Working so that at night, when I lay down there on that hard day bed I could sleep."

"Oh," she said, dropping her head.

"And other times I spent roaming the grounds like a demented sentry, afraid to leave you alone and afraid to stay. You were so lovely, and so heartless."

"Oh, no!"

"Yes!" he insisted. "Do you remember what you said to me? Do you? 'I hope that was satisfactory!'"

"Well, what did you expect," she cried, goaded. "You warned me to resign myself. I thought that lacked something. I still do."

"What did it lack?" he asked, holding out his hand. "Come and tell me."

She wanted the closeness of his arms, and yet, he had not mentioned love. How could she go to him without it? He lay there, strong and vital against the pillows despite his injury. She could feel the attraction of the senses that he had for her, as well as the unconscious domination of his personality. There was about him a touch of the hauteur and leashed strength of the panther in the woods, as well as the black, demonic grace. She had resisted the great cat's primitive domination of predator over prey, by her stillness and the exercise of will. It was possible that if she were resolute enough, she could resist Justin also.

For a long moment she refused the command of his outstretched hand, then, slowly, she moved toward him.

He caught a strand of her honey-gold hair that strayed across her breast. "Claire," he whispered, and pulled her toward him until their lips merged.

"I have loved you since I saw you across that ballroom floor," he told her when at last he released her. "It was not pity, was it, that I saw in your face that night?"

"No, no," she murmured. "It was your scar and the look in your eyes. They hurt me so, and I wanted to do this." She pressed her lips to the crescent that curved down his swarthy cheek.

"Don't!"

She felt his instinctive recoil, even before he spoke.

"Why? It's only a scar."

"It's the mark of a coward," he corrected her with bitterness.

"No," she said deliberately, tracing the curve with a gentle fingertip. "It was never that. Edouard told me it began as the mark of a captive, it was only later, when he could not break your pride, that he taunted you with the other name. But to me it will always stand for courage, the courage of one who took the blame and bore the censure of society, rather than have it fall on a helpless old man. It doesn't matter that it was a mistake. It was real enough for ten long years."

She could feel the tension go out of the facial muscles beneath her fingers, and she smiled. "On the other hand, it could stand for Claire, and I think I rather like having you branded with my initial. A monogrammed husband, just so other women will know to whom to return you."

There was an unconscious plea in her gold-brown eyes, and so retribution was gentle. "Jealous jade," he said, his arm tightening around her, "there will never be a need for it."

At last she struggled free of his grasp. "This is not very comfortable," she said, laughing a little.

"No," he agreed. "Come to bed."

"But you are in my bed."

"So I am. Don't forget to blow out the lamp."

She shook her head, then slowly removed the thin dimity dressing gown with its convent embroidery, and draped it over a chair. Moving to the mirror she picked up her brush and began to brush her hair, separating each long strand.

Suddenly Justin began to laugh. "All right, I did enjoy teasing you in the morning. But you always blushed so beautifully when I caught you watching me. As now. Blow out the lamp, Claire."

"Yes, Justin, in a moment," she said with a promise in her smiling eyes. "In a moment."